Moonbound: The Alpha's Mate

Ariella Nightshade

Contents

Chapter 1

"Sweetie, you have to run! The werewolves will be here soon, we don't stand a chance against them." My father had been trying to convince me to run for the past few minutes.

Then, my mother came in, she looked terrified. "Sylvia, please, run! Our village can't hold them for long when they come!" my mother said.

"I can't leave you guys!" I sobbed. "It was my fault in the first place!"

Just then, there was a faint sound of footsteps.

"Please, run, run until you reach somewhere safe."

I thought about everything. I realized that with me sticking around, they would be more distracted by protecting me rather than themselves. So if I left... they'd have a better chance of survival.

Finally, I nodded. "Please stay safe," I whispered as I gave both of them quick hugs.

Then, I opened our back door, and ran.

I passed through many trees and tripped a few times, got stuck in some sticky mud, but ran all the while. I kept inhaling the sweet forest scent, I never really appreciated it until now, mostly because I rarely went out of the house, unless when hunting food for our village. But that was something else, I had to focus on not getting killed rather than the woody scent of the woods.

Our village was one of the last human ones, it was why we tried our hardest in keeping it secret, but with the wolves' having supernatural abilities, they could sniff us out.

Just right then, I heard a blood-curdling scream, that was when I knew my village was being slaughtered.

And if things couldn't get any worse, I heard fast footsteps or maybe pawsteps behind me.

I didn't bother turning around to know that it was a wolf, I couldn't risk turning around unless I wanted to be caught.

I ran faster, trying not to trip on fallen branches. But even with my hardest efforts, the wolves outran me, after all, they could run very fast, considering that was one of their abilities.

I took the risk to turn around, which was a big mistake. One of the wolves jumped high and landed right on top of me. Its claws extended and slashed on my arm, then, it knocked me unconscious, and everything turned black.

I gasped and felt myself sweating all over. I inhaled, and the scent of rusty metal took over.

I looked around and saw the other humans from my village.

Some of them were untouched, some were injured lightly, while others had bruises all over them.

We were imprisoned in a large cell, just enough for us not to be squished against each other.

Werewolves guarded our cell, near the bars but not too near for them not to touch the silver. I looked around once more, seeing some people unconscious, some even looked dead. But after I looked around the cell the third time, I saw my parents near the wall.

I rushed towards them and hugged them. Relief flooded their eyes when they saw that I wasn't injured much.

I saw that my mom was untouched, but my father had a large wound on his arm, like a claw mark.

The wolves looked like they are debating on whether they make us their slaves, make us fight each other and them watching us as if we were an entertaining TV show, or they would kill us on the spot.

My mother must have seen the worry and concern on my face because she hugged me tighter.

She caressed my back gently, but just right then, one of the werewolves announced, "The Alpha and his Beta will be here shortly, to discuss your fate."

The wolves near him chuckled, while most of us started trembling.

I looked around the room, finding for my friends, I didn't have much friends, since I was barely allowed to go out. It was considered high risk if children were to go out and have fun. We could only go out to hunt for food, and if we made too much noise, the wolves would hear us, they have heightened senses after all.

I looked around the room again, and that's when I finally saw my friends, whispering and clutching each other in fear. Welp, there's my team.

I went over to them, and when they saw me, relief washed their faces. "Sylvia! Thank God you're alive, we thought they chomped you down," Emma said, coming over to hug me.

"Yeah, especially they said if anyone tries running away they'll rip their bodies apart," Ezra said, glaring at one of the nearby wolves. Thankfully, the wolf was on his back, so he didn't see Ezra glare at him, or he'd probably be in pieces right now.

We started chatting, about how we were captured, and how the wolves were so bossy.

The door burst open and a man came out. A powerful aura around him.

An Alpha.

When I looked him in the eye, it was like everything stopped.

And for a moment, I felt lost in them.

Chapter 2

<hr>

I stared at the Alpha's eyes, and I noticed he looked like he was staring at something far away, probably talking to his inner wolf.

The door burst open once more, and two more wolves came from the doorway.

The three of them were the three brothers who ruled the werewolves.

The first one who entered snapped out of it and turned to speak with his brothers. One of his brothers gave me a glance, but when he saw that I noticed, he immediately looked away.

"They look very intimidating," Emma said, not helping my fear at all.

"Hopefully they're not as scary as they look," I muttered.

"Do you think they torture their slaves? They'll probably run out of slaves," Ezra chuckled.

"Not funny, I hope I won't get disposed of."

Our chat was interrupted by someone clearing their throat.

"As you know, we don't take it lightly on humans," Caleb started, he was the middle child and was known to be the one to fix his brothers' problems. I wouldn't have known his name if our chief didn't have some documents about the werewolves and vampires.

He waited for a few moments, to let the words sink in.

I looked around the cell to see most of the people trembling in fear, clutching each other, shaking. I looked over at my friends, they were both looking at the Alpha, fear in their eyes, but they didn't show it through their body posture, they still stood rigidly.

Then, I glanced at my parents, to see they were looking at me, concern and worry overwhelming them. I smiled at them, hoping that would lessen their worry for me. They smiled back, reassuringly.

Caleb glanced around the room, then continued. "But after discussing with my brothers, we decided that we would let you pick - be a slave or death."

The three brothers looked around the room, checking our reactions.

Gasps filled the air since the werewolves were known to usually kill on the spot.

I froze on my spot as I realized that Caine was staring at me.

The three brothers went out of the room, and after a few minutes, the Beta came in.

"Those who wish to be killed instead of slavery, step forward," Beta Jones said in a commanding tone.

Obviously, no one stepped forward, slavery is better than death.

"Alright then, you will all be released later today and will be given specific roles to serve the pack."

With that, he left.

The werewolves that were guarding the cell opened the door to our cell and gave us food and water. But there weren't enough to let all of us eat.

I eagerly grabbed a loaf of bread and a bottle of water and started eating. The others were doing the same except the ones who weren't fast enough.

I was honestly surprised that the Alpha would let all 53 of us serve the pack and not die.

The Alphas went back into the room, and everyone's attention immediately went to them, but when they didn't say anything, everyone started talking again.

Their gazes shifted from one person to another. I ignored their gaze and started a conversation with my friends.

"This is so weird I didn't think they'd make all of us slaves," Emma said, scratching her head.

"Em just be grateful, I'm too young to die," I chuckled.

"I'm curious as to what they'll make us do," Ezra muttered, deep in thought.

"I hope my job isn't too hard," Emma muttered.

"Whatever, you might die before you can do your job."

"Guys stop being negative, you're ruining my positiveness," Ezra said dramatically.

I rolled my eyes and finished eating my loaf of bread and gulped down the rest of the water. I noticed the Alpha's were gone by now.

"All of you will be let out of your cells and can roam around the pack house for an hour - for you to familiarize yourselves in the place, if ever anyone tries to escape, the punishment is death."

After that, Beta Jones opened our cell door with a key and allowed us to go out of the prison.

We all filed out of that rusty place.

"Sylvia, want to stick together?" My friends offered, since I have no sense of direction. I mean, as if they did.

"Yeah sure, just make sure to not get me lost," I chuckled.

"Says the one who always gets lost."

"Shush Em," I scowled.

We were escorted to the main floors of the pack house but just as I was about to go with my friends, Beta Jones stopped me. "Alpha Caine told me that you'll be the one to serve him since the other werewolf who had been serving him retired."

"Eh, okay." He was probably cold and rude, which was why the other one retired, lucky them that they could retire, I'm stuck for life.

"You'll be in the pack house when he doesn't need you, to help the others with their work."

"Okay, okay, sheesh," I mumbled.

He left without saying another word.

I saw my friends staring at me, "What did he say? Are you in trouble?" Emma asked worriedly.

"I'm not in trouble, I have to work for one of the Alpha's and if he doesn't need me I have to work in the pack house, exhausting isn't it?"

"Isn't that better? Maybe you'll get more time-outs?"

"Your not making me feel any better Em."

She rolled her eyes and started walking around, Ezra and I just behind her. Until she bumped into a wolf.

"Back off human," the wolf growled.

"I- erm - s-sorry?" Emma stuttered as the wolf bared its sharp teeth.

Just as it was about to attack Emma, another wolf stepped forward. "We're forbidden to attack any of them unless they try to escape, Coby," the other wolf said.

"The mutt bumped into me!"

"It was an accident," Emma countered, glaring at the wolf.

"Then you admit you all are mutts."

"WHAT?! I didn't-" Emma started.

"You only complained about the bumping part, not the mutt part," the wolf interrupted, giving her a wolfish grin.

Emma glared at the wolf and lead us away. Leaving the two wolves to growl at each other. We went through each room, each hallway, and each staircase, but after all that, we were obviously lost.

Chapter 3

We went around in circles, not knowing where to go and what to do, until Ezra just opened a random door that lead to a hall. The three of us went in, not knowing any other better idea. There were only three rooms in the hall, which made me think... I checked the door again and I saw a sign that said, 'Alpha's Hall'.

"Guys, this is the Alpha's Hall, we're not supposed to be here," I hissed, pointing at the sign.

Both of them stared at me, then Emma said, "I'm curious though, what can be in the Alpha's rooms..."

"No. Don't you dare. Em!" I hissed. Just right then, Caine's door opened. Caine stared at the three of us, then his gaze went on me. Our eyes locked, just like the first time. Then he looked away, staring at Emma who was about to open Carter's door.

"What do you think your doing?" Caine growled.

Emma jumped in surprised, then looked at him, and immediately looked down. "I was curious."

Caine scowled. "This hall is restricted, only my brothers and I can go in, unless we gave you special permission then you are not allowed to get in, you even have the nerve to think of opening my brothers' door!"

"They didn't say we weren't allowed to go in this hall though," Emma muttered.

"How dare you talk back to me!" It was obvious he was pissed. Then, he sighed. "Did you even check the signs?"

"We were lost," Emma squeaked. I was surprised at her nerves.

He sighed then showed us the door.

'Alpha's Hall'

'Do not enter without permission'

"Oh, we were lost, we just went in every door we saw," Emma reasoned, again.

"Don't pretend as if I was not able to hear your conversation," he growled.

He sighed then glanced at the three of us in turn, as if a teacher looking at three hopeless students.

"Get out of here before I change my mind and punish you three."

The three of us turned and sprinted away. Correction, both of them sprinted away.

A hand stopped me from running away from the place.

"Clean my room," I heard Caine grumble. "It hasn't been cleaned ever since the other maid left."

I sighed and turned back, going into their common room and into his room.

He was right, it was like the inside of a trashbin.

But everything still looked expensive.

"Are you going to just stare at my room or start cleaning?"

My face flushed red in embarrassment.

I immediately started fixing his bed, which was really messy. I got the soft, fluffy pillows from the floor and started putting them in place. The creamy sheets were half in the bed and half on the floor. I grabbed the sheets and started putting them back on the bed. I saw Caine staring at me as I fixed his bed. Didn't he have anything better to do?

After I finished fixing his bed, I started putting the misplaced things into order, with Caine's guide of course. Well, he just said where it's supposed to be while watching me clean-up.

After that, he allowed me to finally get the hell out of that place and I sprinted downstairs, then bumped into a wolf.

Just my luck

"I'm sorry, I didn't mean to bump into you."

"Its fine, do you need something?" The wolf asked.

"Umm, I'm lost... do you mind helping me go to the main floor?"

"That's not a problem, anyways my name's Trix, yours?" She said as she started guiding me through the hallways.

"Sylvia, nice to meet you."

"Ohhh your the girl that Alpha Caine requested to be his maid," she said, smiling.

"So that's how I'll be known now, 'the girl Alpha Caine requested to be his maid'," I muttered, not too fond of it. Requested wasn't probably the word that fit, it was more like 'demanded'.

"Yeah well, the Alpha's never risked having a human servant, they always get the wolves to be the ones serving them."

"Ohh," I should really dig more info.

"Anyways we're here, just ask the guy over there for what you have to do."

"Thanks, Trix!"

"It's really not a problem," she smiled, then walked away.

I walked towards the 'guy' she pointed to and he smiled, "I'm assuming you're here for what you need to do."

I nodded.

"Most of the spots are already taken but... we do need some help in the kitchen." He started leading me to a huge kitchen and motioned for me to go with the other girls making dinner. And that's where I went.

They looked at me and smiled, "Here to help?" One of them asked.

"Mhm," I replied.

Then we started making the food, while talking of course, and it was kind of fun getting to know each other.

"I'm also from your village you know, but I barely got friends since my mom wouldn't let me out."

"Yeah, they were scared that the wolves would come after us."

"I kinda like it better in here."

"Mhm."

After a few minutes of talking, werewolves started piling into the dining hall, and we started giving them the food and drinks, which they eagerly grabbed.

Most of the wolves were friendly; I regret judging all of them just because one of their kind killed my grandmother.

Some snarled and held their chin up like royalty as they grabbed the food.

Some were suspicious of us and sniffed the food in case we poisoned it.

"Brown-haired girl! Alpha has been waiting for you to bring his food up to his room!" One of the wolves informed me.

"Oh okay, I'll be up there in a sec."

The wolf walked towards the food section without another word.

Chapter 4

I grabbed a tray but I realized I didn't know what the Alpha liked to eat.

I tapped a random wolf's shoulder.

Big mistake.

It was the same wolf, the one who called humans mutts.

He slowly turned around and glared at me.

"What do you want?" He growled.

Sheesh, so moody.

"Nothing, sheesh, I was just going to ask if you knew what the Alpha usually eats."

"Which Alpha? Meh, doesn't matter, they all have the same favorite, baked garlic chicken parmesan," he pointed to the dish served on different plates.

Then smiled.

That dude actually smiled.

Well, let me take my words back.

He smiled to show his sharp canines.

I rolled my eyes. I got a random unused tray and piled four baked garlic chicken parmesans on it. Well, wolves have a high appetite right? I put six more.

Do wolves get thirsty a lot? Well, I don't really care but I don't want to go back and forth so I just got three bottles of water.

I re-counted the parmesans, just in case.

I don't want to look like a fool going back and forth from their room and to the kitchen.

I got up the stairs, went through hallways, and opened random doors, because, well, no one told me where exactly the Alpha's Hall was. Even though I got there the first time, I don't know how to get there the second time.

After what seemed like forever, I finally found the door with the Alpha's Hall sign.

I slowly twisted the doorknob, then peeked in.

I squinted my eyes to see through the small dent.

The two eldest Alphas sat on the white modular sofa, talking about things I couldn't quite hear.

Seeing that I couldn't get a snoop of anything, I just opened the door wider, and both their heads snapped in my direction.

It wasn't like I heard anything.

I raised one of my eyebrows.

"I brought food for Alpha Caine," I said, holding the tray out.

Caleb looked from the tray to Caine.

"Don't tell me all your muscles are from fats," Caleb said, staring at the piled-up parmesans. His lips closed tight telling me that he was trying to stifle a laugh.

Caine's mouth opened then closed.

"I eat even less than half of that!" Caine countered, glaring at his brother.

"Doubt it, have a nice time," he said, waving before going into his room and slamming the door shut.

Caine and I had a small staring contest before I finally looked away, staring at the rug with a 'welcome' sign instead.

He opened the door of his room and motioned for me to get in. I was honestly surprised it was how I left it, I thought it would turn even messier than before.

I placed the tray on a random table and was about to leave the room when Caine stopped me with an arm.

"You brought too much food for me."

So? "Sorry? I'll just put it back downstairs then."

"No it's fine, eat with me instead," he offered.

Eat with you? No thanks.

"Umm, okay."

I stared at the one seat pushed into the hole of the table. Was I going to eat while standing?

As if he had heard my thoughts, he pulled a random chair from the common room and put it near the table, waiting for me to sit.

Aren't I supposed to be the one to serve?

I slowly sat down, staring at the wall filled with pictures while Caine sat on the other chair.

I blinked as he messily tore the parmesan with his teeth.

Then he looked up.

"Well? What are you waiting for? Eat."

My nose scrunched up slightly, I wasn't really used to someone ordering me around, except for our village chief giving orders around, but it was for our own safety. I still ate anyway. I didn't want to get into a powerful werewolf's bad side.

I looked through his wall filled with pictures while eating. Especially the funny ones, like where he opened his mouth with his fingers, sticking his tongue out at the camera, but it was when he was younger, so it was cute rather than funny.

Caine's eyes went from my eye to the picture I was looking at and sighed.

"Always that picture, I should take it down soon," he muttered under his breath.

I almost let out a chuckle, but I stopped myself before I could.

He was an Alpha, a powerful one.

While I was just a human, probably a little insect he can squish then I'll go 'poosh', gone.

I've never felt this inferior to someone before. I guess it was because of the shelter I was provided, I think I've gotten too used to how I was before, free. Carefree, cheerful, and happy. I wanted my freedom, but I knew it wasn't possible.

I finished five parmesans in just 2 minutes. I know, amazing, aren't I?

I haven't eaten such good food in months, or maybe half a year, and now, it was served on a silver platter. And, of course, I'd gladly take the opportunity.

Caine was watching me with his watchful eyes. From how I ate the food, to how I awkwardly coughed each time he stared at me. It was very disturbing.

After he finished eating, he gave me simple instructions.

Just to get the food down, leave it for the others to wash, eat dessert, if I want to, then just go to my dorm room.

I got the tray, with the leftover crumbs of parmesan, and the empty bottles and went straight out of the room. That was pretty creepy and stalky if you ask me.

I stumbled down the stairs, not being able to hold the handle with either hand since both hands were being used.

I finally got down the stairs and left the dishes in the sink, throwing the empty plastic bottles in the bin.

And, since I was allowed to eat dessert, I took a strawberry frozen yogurt from the fridge. I mean, no one would waste this opportunity. Unless they're allergic, and that sucks.

I glanced around the dining hall, looking for Emma or Ezra anywhere.

So far, they were the only ones I knew anyway.

"Over here," I heard Emma's chirpy voice from my right.

I turned around and saw her waving her arms, as if trying to attract my attention.

Well, that did it.

I walked over to her table and sat down, twisting the cover of the yogurt's sealed cup.

I ate a spoonful of yogurt and then turned to look at Emma to start a conversation, but that was when I noticed a wolf on her lap.

That was so not normal.

We used to be so scared of wolves, we tried to not even be heard or seen by them.

Used to be.

Now that we were in a house, or a mansion rather, filled with more than a hundred werewolves.

And some were actually nice.

Maybe I was just being paranoid about the whole thing, maybe werewolves weren't that bad, I mean, they are still half human anyway.

"Who's that?" I asked, gesturing my spoon to the brownish-black wolf she was holding.

"Guess who," she said with a grin.

"Uhm, the guy who called humans mutts?"

I was really bad at guessing.

"Nope, it's Ezra, they recruited all the men from our village who they think could survive the shift, there's this part they bite," she gestured to her neck. "Then after that, Ez told me they made them drink some sort of potion that burned his insides, they said it was to skip the transitioning and poof into a werewolf immediately, but with consequences."

I raised one eyebrow in curiosity.

"They have to shift four times a day for a whole month, and Ez says it really hurts when shifting. They say that the shifts will come naturally after the side effects stop working."

"Oh, well," I said as I finished my yogurt. "Sucks to be him."

The wolf snapped its head up.

"Totally," Em said, patting Ezra's furry head. "By the way, they gave our dorm numbers while you were serving the Alpha, I made sure to take note of yours, it's room 07."

"Alright, I'll see you soon I guess," I said, walking away to place the cup and disposable spoon in the trash bin.

Chapter 5

Room 29... ugh this is gonna take a while.

I walked past the other rooms until I finally stumbled across my room. I grabbed my key and opened it, hoping that my roommate wouldn't be as bad as the 'mutt' guy.

As I opened the door, I was surprised to see Trix.

"Hi V," Trix said with a smile, she smiled at me briefly before continuing to type on her computer.

"V?" I asked. "Oh wait, why are you here? I thought they were separating wolves and humans."

"They mixed the wolves and humans, so yeah, we're room-mates," she explained.

Before I could interrupt, she continued, "Because," she cleared her throat. "One, the wolves could protect themselves if ever the humans try something— not that I think you're going to try something," she immediately added when she saw the look on my face.

"And, two, the wolves won't try anything, unless they want to become rogue, it can get them killed, so nothing to worry about," she said, shrugging her shoulders as if it were nothing.

I shrugged and took a moment to look around.

We both had the same beds with a brown-ish rug patterned with different stripes of brown on it. A small wooden table sat beside each of our beds, the one that I'm assuming was mine had some books on top of it. A creamy curtain was just right in between the room, it was opened right now, it was probably made for us to have some privacy.

A door stood just around the corner, most probably the bathroom, where I was heading.

I twisted the doorknob and went in. I opened the shower and started scrubbing.

After I finished, I literally wrecked the whole place by trying to find where the towels were.

Finally, in the last cupboard I opened, I found four fluffy white towels. I grabbed one of them, then, dried and covered myself. I changed into one of the most comfortable pj's I could find.

Luckily, they provided us with clothing, because basically, we were under their protection. And the clothing they provided was much more comfortable than the ones I normally had at home. Maybe living with wolves weren't so bad after all.

I hopped onto my bed and looked over at Trix. She was already preparing to sleep, cleaning her desk and turning her computer off. I looked over to the wooden table next to me. I touched one of the book covers. Trix didn't have books on hers, probably because she wasn't new? I checked the title of the one with a gray leather cover. 'The Ancient Wolves'

Hmmm, interesting.

I'll probably read it tomorrow after work. I didn't bother checking the covers of the other two books because soon after, I fell asleep.

I woke up to the sound of an alarm clock ringing. No, it's not my alarm clock. It was Trix'. And it seemed like she was running late because she still hasn't woken up yet.

Wasn't really my business but I liked waking people up.

I walked over to her and started shaking, pinching, and slapping her to wake her up. I even tried looking for her tickly spot and put the ringing alarm in her ear.

One last choice then.

It was the worse for the victim and best for the attacker.

Mind you, this is my favorite way of waking someone up.

I slowly walked into the bathroom, as if giving her the 'last chance' to wake up.

I got a random empty vase that didn't even have flowers or plants or whatever wolves put it in vases and filled it with some water. I went back to her and splashed the whole thing on her sleeping figure.

"What the-," she screamed before she got a glimpse of her alarm clock.

"Oh shit, I'm late, gotta go, thanks but no thanks for your waking technique," Trix said before dashing into the shower to take a quick bath.

Honestly, I wasn't sure what I was supposed to do, so I just took the same book that I saw last night and placed it on my lap.

I flipped through the pages until I found something that caught my eye. A picture of Caine and his brothers, a black and white picture. Before I could look down at the description, Emma burst into the room. Uninvited.

"What are you doing in here?

"You need to get working right now, Caine has been asking for his breakfast fifteen minutes ago." She panted, she had obviously ran up all the way here.

I immediately bolted up from bed and rushed down the stairs with Emma without another word. I bolted in the kitchen, grabbed a tray, filled it with food grabbed a random drink and rushed up the stairs to where the Alpha's lived in.

But just as I was about to open the door I overheard the Alphas talking, and my hand froze.

"Should we have the other humans changed?"

"It might be risky... but we also need backup. The vampires are trying to take over," another voice said.

"We already turned some of the boys but I'm not sure about the rest," a voice that I recognized that was Caine's.

I tried peeking from the white door, which was a mistake because they all stared at me. Anger is evident in their eyes. So I thought of the most logical thing to do. Open the door and state my business, and be done with it. But it didn't really go as planned.

As soon as I placed the tray on their common room table, Carter pushed me towards the ground and held a fist near my face. I tried to wriggle free from his grasp, but of course, he was too strong for me.

"Eavesdropping isn't nice you know, especially when it's about something you shouldn't know about."

Chapter 6

I was pinned onto the wall with Carter's hands. I stared into his sky blue eyes, though his eyes started deepening in color, turning pitch black after a few moments. He growled at me. "I said, how much have you heard?!"

"E-enough to hear about the vampires thing?" I answered nervously, I mean, even if I lied they would've known anyway.

He sighed and glared at me. He looked as if he was about to punch me when Caine literally strangled his brother. I stared at them in shock.

What surprised me even more was...

...Caleb staring at them as if this was a show.

"What are you doing? Stop them! Pssst," I hissed at Caleb. He just looked at me, then a smirk tugged on the corner of his lips, "Nah, their always like that."

"Do something!" I practically screamed, "They're fighting each other!"

"Someone concerned about their ma-," he immediately cut himself short, realizing it wasn't his place to tell.

I hissed and said another quick "C'mon, do something?" As the two brothers punched each other, Caine's punch landing on Carter's jaw while Carter's landing on his shoulder.

Caleb smirked at me one last time before whipping out two daggers from his pocket, then lashed it out to both his brothers at lightning speed.

I stared at him like he was crazy.

He blinked innocently, "You told me to stop them."

Good point.

"But not like that-," I was cut short by a dagger literally pulled off Carter's stomach and thrown right at Caleb, but what shocked me most was that the dagger stopped inches short from his chest.

"H-how- what?" I stuttered.

He explained it in one single word.

"Telekinesis."

My jaw nearly dropped to the ground and my eyes looked like they were about to pop out of their sockets.

"So you guys aren't just wolves?" I asked. My brain was filled with thousands of questions right now, that I want answered.

"That's enough information you've learned now," Caine growled, shoving the dagger from his knee and putting it on the table.

Carter was just glaring at me. Then, he shoved me out of the room. I immediately took the chance to run. I went downstairs to check if I needed to do anything but they said all spots were occupied so— more free time for me!

I went to my room and plopped down to my bed. Then, I opened the gray leather covered book and flipped through the pages until I found the one from a while ago morning. I checked the description.

'The three brothers are not only ancient werewolves, they were also pure bloods and are capable of magic, they were cursed by a witch to never find their mates, because of their cruelty. But little did she know that once she did, her magic transferred itself to them.'

Pure Bloods? Ancient werewolves? I need to know more.

Just as I was about to flip through more pages, a knock sounded on the door. Who could that be?

"Come in!" I called.

The doorknob twisted open and Caine went in. I was surprised to have seen him.

"Ummm, I'm sorry about earlier," I said softly, the guilt finally kicking in.

"Actually, it's fine. I came to apologize, we shouldn't have put a— how would you call it? A show." Caine said, scratching his head.

"But you guys were the one who got hurt— because I bugged in and heard something I shouldn't have," I said, barely above a whisper.

Caine laughed, as if it were a joke. "You should really know that we fight a lot. Plus as a werewolf, we heal easily."

"Some werewolf healing magic?" I asked, curiously.

"If that's how you call it," he replied. "Anyways, I'll see you soon, I only came to apologize. I still have some work to do." And with that, he was out in a flash. I just shrugged and started flipping through more pages. I gasped as I finally found what I was looking for.

The Pureblooded Werewolves

Pure bloods are known to be stronger, faster and have more heightened senses. They could hide their scent from other wolves, but they have to know how to do it. Pureblooded werewolves are known to be rare, as they were always sought out to be killed, or to be imprisoned to do their bidding. In shorter words, they are more powerful and more valuable than normal wolves.

Rank in packs:

They are more protected as well as more respected than normal wolves. They are more or less equal to the rank of a Delta, though if that Delta is not a pure blood, the pure bloods are more powerful than the third in command.

At least I got my answers, but how to know if its a normal wolf or not? Gosh I'm filled with questions now. I closed the book with a loud 'thud' and placed it back on the table.

I went out the door into the kitchen. By the time I got in there, Emma and the others were halfway done in making lunch. When she saw me, she said, "Don't help us in here, Caine asked you to go fix their common room, he said its a mess."

The guilt crept back to me. But I was curious on how Emma keeps knowing when Caine actually needs something from me. So I asked, "How do you always know when he needs me to do something?"

"I'm a wolf, we use mind link."

Chapter 7

Shock was written all across my face. Emma, Em was a wolf. Questions overwhelmed my mind once more.

How?

When?

I just learned some things about Pureblooded Werewolves and now this...?

"I got turned, like, almost right away when we got... you know.." Emma said softly. "Then these wolves taught me how to control it and stuff so yeah."

"Anyways, you better get to Caine now or he's going to kill you," she chuckled.

I smiled and rushed towards their room. I opened the door to find the three brothers, sitting on one of the coaches. Staring at me.

Isn't this so awkward?

Caine cleared his throat. Right. I'm supposed to clean...

I started picking up the small shreds from the vases they threw, I winced when my finger started bleeding. "You don't do it like that," Caine muttered. "Just sweep it off the floor." He pointed towards the broom and dustpan. I hummed in response and grabbed it, cleaning the rest of the room, while they just stared at me. Which was kind of awkward but its fine.

After they dismissed me, I went back to my room that I shared with Trix. I opened the door and started finding for a first aid kit to bandage my bleeding finger. I checked the small drawers near the bathroom door and found a small, red, first aid kit with the words 'Room 07' embroidered in it. I zipped the zipper open and grabbed some bandages, then wrapped it around my finger. Yes, I know I'm being kind of dramatic in here, but I'm kind of scared of blood.

After that, I went back downstairs. The others were supposed to be eating right now. I went over to where the slaves and servants usually eat, and found Anna, Emma and Ezra eating at their usual table. They waved me over and I smiled as I saw a reserved spot beside Anna. I went over to them and dug into the food they got for me. "Thanks for the reserve," I murmured as I dug into my yogurt. They got me a strawberry flavored one. My favorite.

"Your always welcome."

I smiled at them. They were just the best friends ever. Don't get me wrong— I'm not using them. I ate the rest of my food and drank the rest of my water while chatting with my friends.

But then I loud 'bang' and the doors opening caught our attention. Well, everyone's attention, really. I looked over at the main thing and saw a werewolf holding a human as if he weighed like a feather. There were more werewolves behind him. Then, the guy holding the human spoke. "As a warning for all of you not try to escape, we will be punishing this human," he indicated towards the human he was holding, "that tried escaping."

I stared in horror and fear as they started whipping the man as if he was a horse. I was really scared if the man will make it alive. The werewolf didn't care, he just whipped with all his might. I can't believe they don't even show mercy... I feel so bad yet I can't do anything about it. I hope my father wouldn't be stupid enough to try to escape... the punishment... it's not worth it.

I watched them whip the guy, watched as every bloody wound was placed. I watched as the blood dried out of him. As he cried in pain and begged for mercy. And no, the wolves didn't show mercy. They laughed hysterically as if it was some weird joke. I honestly felt like slapping the guy right now. And without even noticing what I was doing, I was walking up to them. Anna and the others tried stopping me. But no. I couldn't do this. He didn't deserve this for just trying to escape. To try and get a freedom everyone deserved. But what did he get? A punishment that could get him killed. I can't watch as these werewolves slaughtered the life out of the man.

And when I was facing him. I slapped him. Right in the face. I watched as his face morphed to anger.

"Who are you to do that?" He growled fiercely, as if it were a warning.

There was no backing down now.

I took in a deep breath and said, "You can't just slaughter him like that then laugh like a maniac in here. You can't punish someone so highly just because they're trying to seek for their own freedom and want their actual life back then. You won't ever, and I mean ever, understand how us humans feel because you never were one. You're already punishing him, and you make him feel like he's not worth anything by how you laugh with your little werewolf friends there. Just because you guys are stronger and more powerful doesn't mean you can trample over everyone and everything that gets in your way, thats just selfish."

He and his werewolf friends just stared at me. Well, everyone stared at me actually. I mentally gulped, knowing there would be a punishment after what I have said but... someone's gotta spit facts in them. And no one had the nerve to do that so— I just did it.

"You do know you'll get severely punished by me after what you did," he growled. He was pissed. Anyone can tell.

"Yes but someone had to stop you before the guy dies," I replied, glaring at him.

"I can easily beat a human," he growled, louder this time. Then, he took one step forward. I had to do a whole load of pep talk in my mind to not step back.

Then, without warning, he lunged at me and whispered four words in my ear. Four words that sent chills down my spine. Four words.

"You'll regret this, human."

Chapter 8

After the words left the werewolf's mouth, I suddenly thought about all the possible things he could do to me. Since I was still pinned on the wall, he could torture or even kill me. Fear bubbled in my insides. Will he bite me everywhere until I die? Stab me? Whip me like he did to the guy? What will he do?! Without noticing, I was trembling and shaking. The werewolf raised the whip and was about to whip me when he was suddenly thrown to the ground.

By Caine.

My eyes literally popped out of its sockets when Caine punched the guy. Everyone was staring, feeling as shocked as I am. Like why would Caine even help me? I slapped and talked back to him. He has every right to be angry— at the slap part. But I doubt that he even felt it, for one, I think I was the one who got hurt by slapping him. His face was as hard as stone!

Caine was talking to the guy, and I actually feel bad for him. He looked so scared and his face showed pure terror.

Who wouldn't be scared of Caine? He's an Alpha, higher rank, more powerful, stronger and who knows what else? Caleb has telekinesis- what can he do? At this point, I don't even think I want to know. But still, I have the right to be curious. I winced as the man struggled to get back on his feet.

I couldn't watch this any longer. And so I opened the doors leading to the exit and went up my room. I didn't have anything else to do so I just took a warm bath and started flipping through the same gray leather covered book, learning more about werewolves until I'd have to do something I guess.

So... basically Caine and his brothers have magic?! Like how crazy is that? I almost feel bad for the man that he was beating up earlier. But them that could have been me. Call me selfish but I can't help it. I'm not ready to die. I plopped down to bed and flipped through the pages.

I opened the door to the Alpha's rooms quietly, and I placed the tray filled with food on Caine's desk. Then, I went back down the stairs, going to my friends' usual table and started eating my lasagna. I listened in their conversation until it dropped to me.

"Sylvia, don't you think its weird that Caine did what he did a while ago?" Anna asked, shifting the topic. I almost jumped in surprise.

"I don't know? What did he do?" I feel stupid for saying that. He just saved my life.

"He threatened the werewolf guy to never touch you again," Emma explained, pointing her fork to me for more effect.

I choked on my lasagna and stared at the now very interesting floor.

"Do you think...?" Emma said, giggling like a girl. She is a girl.

"No!" I practically screamed, feeling my cheeks redden at the thought. "He's an alpha and I'm just his slave that does everything he wants, nothing else," I said, trying to clear the thought from their minds.

"Yeah. Sure." Anna said, grinning like an idiot. Meanwhile, Emma was making 'oooooh' sounds while smirking.

I glared at them. "If you two seriously think— I don't know what to do with you guys anymore," I muttered.

"You left before you heard what he was saying so— you wouldn't know why we're totally shipping you two!" Emma squealed.

"If you two think that the two— alpha and a slave, can be together, then I don't think you guys can get any dumber."

"Hmph," Emma pouted, crossing her arms across her chest.

I laughed as I finished the rest of my lasagna and drank some water. "I'll see you guys tomorrow, good night," I said to them before I went to my room.

After all that happened on this day, I fell asleep almost immediately.

I yawned and stretched my arms. But when I opened my eyes, I literally screamed. There was a butterfly on my nose.

A large brown butterfly. Trix jolted awake when she heard me, thinking it was something important. Then, she laughed. "Are you seriously afraid of a butterfly?"

"Perhaps, perhaps not."

"Butterflies aren't supposed to be scary."

"They're insects!"

She sighed, talking about humans and their fear for such little innocent insects. Well, who could blame me for being scared of them? It appeared on my nose, right after I woke up. Or has it been standing there since I fell asleep? I don't even want to think about it. Slowly, I tried shoving it away. But, after deciding it would be better to give it to chance and make it shoo willingly, I waved my hand around my nose, and, as if on cue, it gracefully flew away. Finally.

I went onto doing my morning routine, and since it was too early, I went downstairs to grab some chips in the kitchen. You may think that we are 'stuck' here and that we are slaves and all, but they're actually pretty nice to us, and I'm grateful for that.

I grabbed a bag of chips and went back up the stairs, I opened the door to my room and sat on my bed. I grabbed the same gray covered book and flipped it open, wanting to have my questions answered.

Chapter 9

- -

I flipped through the pages as I crunched through my chips. Honestly, I don't know what I was looking for, I think what I wanted to do was kill my time. But I didn't have to wait for long, because Trix' alarm clock soon went off. I stood from my bed, slowly. I was clean and dressed, so I have no need to hurry, unlike Trix. I closed the book with a loud 'thud' and stood up. Then, I went downstairs, deciding to help the others in making breakfast. It was a good thing I did because there were less people doing the chores today.

Out of curiosity, I decided to ask one of my fellow workers about this.

"Most of them went training, they said something about having to learn self-defense," was her answer.

Was is something about the vampires I had heard of? I hope not! Vampires were the most greedy creatures I have ever known of. They were even worse than the wolves, if ever I had to choose a side- werewolf or vampire, I'd definitely take the werewolf's side. They are much nicer and they at least don't turn random humans into werewolves. I heard the reason on why there were so little humans left was because vampires has turned any human they have seen into a vampire. Vampires didn't care whether or not they get hurt in war, because their basically dead already.

"What about you?" I asked.

"We take turns in lessons, well, some of us have to stay behind and do the work after all, and some of us aren't turned yet," she answered.

After making breakfast, I grabbed a tray and filled it with food, going to Caine's room. He looked stressed, staring at a bunch of papers as he examined them, reading each word thoroughly. He looked so focused that I mentally debated whether or not to give him the food. I mentally slapped my forehead. Of course I should, it's my job to give him food and do whatever he wanted. I gently placed the tray on a part of his desk that wasn't filled with papers.

He looked at me, "Do you want to change into a werewolf?"

That question wasn't the kind I was expecting. "I don't know," I answered truthfully. He seemed to have been expecting a yes or no answer. He stood up and walked in front of me. "I need an answer, I can give you a day's time but no longer. We're running out of time and... I'm worried for your safety. I need to know if you want to turn into a werewolf, by any chance, so that you can protect yourself."

What he said had me surprised, he cared for me? He was worried for my safety? Why? I am just a mere servant.

"I-is this about the vampires?" I asked out of pure curiosity.

He looked at my eyes, as if he was trying to read my soul. "Yes. They might be planning an attack sooner or later, and I want you to be safe."

"Oh," was all I could get out of my throat.

"Chances of us losing are high, they have taken a lot of humans and changed them into vampires, even before they hated us," he said as he glanced back down at the papers.

I didn't really know any vampires that were after me so I don't think I have anything to worry about. For now.

After he allowed me to leave, I left. I went in my room and started thinking whether or not should I be turned into a werewolf.

I was listing the pro's and con's in being a werewolf. Shifting into a werewolf during the full moon was one of the most painful things ever, and the urge to kill during the full moon... who knows what things I would do? Then again if I was a werewolf, I could defend myself when the time comes... so I decided I would become a werewolf.

I walked over to Caine's room, opened the door to his room to find him staring at me.

"I knew you'd come sooner or later," he said with a smile. "What's your decision?"

"I want to turn into a werewolf."

He looked shocked at what I said but he nodded. "Alright, when?"

"As soon as possible, I want to know ho to defend myself from those crazy blood suckers," I said with a smile on my face. He smiled at me, not one of those crazy insane smiles people give, no. It was a genuine sweet smile.

"Are you sure? Wolves go through a very painful process each full moon. Only my brothers and I can control the transition."

My eyes widened at what he said. He and his brothers can control the transition?! "Yeah, I already know about that, but you and your brothers can control the transition?" I said softly.

He nodded. "Don't worry about wolves killing each other though, we lock ourselves all wolves up, except me and my brothers, every full moon because on that same day, the vampires have more thirst for blood."

"So if you let them go, they kill each other?" I squeaked in realization.

He nodded and looked at me. "Are you sure you really want to?" He asked.

"Yes, I really want to," I said softly. What will become of me after this transformation?

"Tomorrow, we will do it tomorrow," he answered. I nodded and left the room.

Chapter 10

The night of the full moon has come. The first full moon I will be spending as a wolf. "Lock yourself up in the basement," Caine had said. He told me it will hold me off, so that I would be able to stay in the pack house for the night. But I didn't, I didn't want to lock myself up. That night I grew restless. I started transforming into a wolf. The very first time I would be able to do the transformation.

But little did I know, once I have fully transformed, I suddenly had the urge to kill. To kill everyone in my path. I was restless, I jumped out of the window and into the woods. I started finding for someone to be my prey. But then, a vampire appeared. "Ah, a little disobedient wolf," he said, a menacing smile on his face. I growled at him but he just patted me and took me in his arms. I wanted to bite him, attack him. But I could do nothing of the sort. The man smiled at me then pointed to a human. Suddenly, my urges to kill heightened. I leapt towards the human girl and attacked. I didn't know what I was doing until it was done.

I woke up, panting, sweat filled my forehead. I looked around, this was the day I was going to be turned to a werewolf. Do I really want this? What would happen if I accidentally killed someone just like I had in the dream?

I'll be fine as long as I do what the other wolves do. But I still feel scared for whatever t will happen. It's just a bite but the transformation... I might kill someone by accident, but as long as I do what Caine says I won't do anything wrong, right?

Yeah I'll be good.

I walked out of my room and went through flights of stairs. I was planning to ask Caine what to do but when I reached the door, I heard voices.

"No. Your not the one that's going to turn her."

"Yes. I'll be the one to turn her! What if the other wolf messes up? She's my mate!"

"It's unfair for the others, she's just a normal slave."

My heart skipped a beat. Were they talking about me? My heart started picking up a pace and I started sweating.

"She's my mate; therefore she's my equal."

After those words, I accidentally knocked off a vase, but I caught it in time. God, my clumsiness. I immediately put it back in place. I didn't want to get caught, so I left. But after a few minutes, I went back there, this time, I didn't waste any time and opened the door. And once I did, I found all three brothers staring at me. Welp, this is awkward.

"Uhh," I stammered. Okay, I just realized I don't know what to say. Oh well.

"Just get on with it, brother," Carter said through clenched teeth.

Caine walked over to me, then grabbed my hand and let me sit on one of the leather coaches. I could feel sparks on where our hands touched. I had to shut my mouth to not let out a satisfied sigh.

"Are you sure you want to do this?" Caine asked.

"Y-yes," I tried my best to not make my voice shaky but I was nervous.

"Alright then..."

He leaned close to my neck, so close that I could feel his hot breath on it. He opened his mouth and elongated his canines. Then, he plunged a hole on my neck, letting the substance in his canines sink through my neck. That was all I remembered until everything turned black.

When I opened my eyes, the first thing I noticed was that my eyesight was way clearer. Then I heard some conversations in the hallway. I'm officially an eavesdropper.

Hi human, a voice inside my head said.

Umm, hi? Who are you? Get out of my head.

I'm basically you. I'm your wolf.

Oh yeah. I forgot I was basically a werewolf. Oh.

Humans are dumber than I thought, the wolf said.

I glared at it. The door burst open and Caine went in. "Thank God your awake."

"What?"

"I thought I did it wrong!" He said.

I wasn't paying any more attention to whatever he was saying because my wolf won't stop talking in my head.

Isn't mate charming?

Excuse me?

Caine's our mate! He's the cutest thing!

Keep dreaming.

I'm telling the truth! He's our mate! And he sure is hot...

I mentally snarled at my wolf, who kept rambling about Caine. But the real Caine stared at me. "Uhh I think your wolf is bugging you then?" He asked with a grin.

I nodded.

I'm not bugging you!

Yes you are.

Hmph! If I stop talking, you'd feel like you lost your other half.

I doubt it but I kind of enjoyed my wolf blabbing around.

"Caine?" I said.

"Hmm?" He asked, letting me go on.

"What did my wolf say about mates?"

When I had said that he jumped. "What did she say?"

"She said your my mate, I don't get it," I said honestly.

A mate is someone you're destined to love forevermore, my wolf said happily.

Chapter 11

"**N**ow you know then, this is the reason on why my brothers didn't want to turn you into a werewolf," Caine said as sat down beside me.

Meanwhile, my wolf in my head grew ecstatic on our mate sitting close to us.

"Oh, so what exactly is a mate?" I asked.

I didn't really know if my wolf was lying or not. But she probably isn't since she said she was my other 'half'.

"Like a soulmate, you should really check out the books I placed on your bedside table," he chuckled.

"Your the one who placed the books there?"

"Yes, who else?" He said with a smile.

"Well, I'll get on with reading then," I said as I stood up and left the room. That was when I realized that I was on his room a few seconds ago. I walked out of their common room and left the Alpha's Hall. I went through several hallways and staircases until I finally reached my own room. I opened the door and went in. Trix was on the edge of her bed, looking very worried. When she saw me, she quickly stood and ran to give me a hug.

"I was so worried! I thought you weren't able to survive the transformation!" Trix said, her coice laced with concern.

"Yeah, I, um, passed out after Caine bit me," I muttered.

"Caine was the one who bit you?!" Trix asked in surprise.

"Umm yeah?" I said.

Her eyes widened and she smirked. "Hmmm what does your wolf say about him?"

"W-what? N-n-nothing!" I stammered.

We shouldn't be ashamed of our mate, my wolf said, scowling at me through my head.

I never said I was.

You act like it. Anyways back to mate...

Then she started blabbering about him again, it was annoying to be honest.

"Hmmm?" Trix said again.

"It's nothing, really," I murmured

"Anyways, you should go rest for now, having to turn into a werewolf isn't an easy process," with that, she left the room.

I jumped into bed and relaxed my head on the headboard. Then, I grabbed the books that Caine had so kindly put on my nightstand. I looked at the covers. 'The Ancient Werewolves', 'Mates', 'All you need to know about Vampires'

Well, it was obvious it was the 'Mates' one I needed. I flipped in the pages and started reading.

Mates are the true love of each wolf. Wolves find their specific mate when they turn to the age of eighteen, but some are unfortunate and find their mate at an older age. Mates are basically the other half of a wolf, without each other, the other is like an empty shell, without the capability of loving or having any feelings for anyone else.

So, this book is saying that Caine was my other half?!

Yes, that's exactly what it is, human.

I wasn't asking you, I was asking myself.

Don't be bitchy, I'm trying to be nice here.

Mk, fine, sorry?

It's fine! My wolf said chirpily.

So, whoever is a person's mate is stuck with the mate forever? You can't reject them or something?

My wolf gasped at this. What? Your thinking of rejecting our mate?!

No. I meant-

But she already left my mind. I feel bad for that, it was mainly my fault. I was thinking of asking Caine about when our wolf leaves our mind but he probably has too much in his hair now so... okay never mind I'm going to ask him. I went to the room that he and his brothers' shared and was about to go in his room when Carter grabbed my shoulder.

"I wouldn't disturb him if I were you."

"Mkay," I muttered.

"Why do you need to talk to him?" He asked, sitting down on one of the beanbag chairs.

"My wolf blocked me in my head, I was just curious."

He nearly choked on what he was drinking. "Are you so annoying that your wolf blocked you on your first day with it?"

I glared at him, "I was just asking if there was no way we could reject a mate and don't have to be stuck with that person forever."

"You want to WHAT?! What did my brother do wrong?" His eyes nearly popped out of its sockets as he started shaking me by my shoulders.

"N-no I w-was just c-curious," I said as he stopped shaking me.

"Don't even dare to think about rejecting my brother, he never thought he had a mate and he was the one who forced us to not kill that village of yours," he growled.

"Never thought he had a mate?" I echoed.

"Yes, we're cursed, now you know," he muttered.

"Cursed?"

Honestly, I feel dumb echoing whatever Carter was saying.

"Yes, are you slow?"

I scowled at him and looked away. But then the door to Caine's room burst open. "Were you talking about rejecting me?!" He said in alarm.

Then, he started shaking me just like Carter did. "Did I do something wrong? What did I do to make you want to reject me?"

"N-no I w-was j-just curious," I stammered.

He stopped shaking me and ran a hand across his hair and started taking deep breaths.

"Umm, the reason I came here is because I wanted to ask about my wolf," I began.

"She- er, blocked me out or something," I muttered.

"You can't transform if she does that," Carter pointed out.

That was the last thing I needed to know, I just wanted to know if my wolf was okay.

I'm fine! I just needed a break and now I'm back! My wolf was chirpy as usual, and that made me smile.

The two brothers noticed my smile and had probably guessed that my wolf was back, so they just left me in their common room.

But just then, I felt two hands grab my body. A few more dark figures went up from the window, and just as I was about to scream, the man behind me put a handkerchief on my nose and was I inhaled it's scent, I fell unconscious.

Chapter 12

I blinked my eyes and was surprised to see that I was back in a cell. I felt cold, and the cold, rusty floor was making it worse. I inhaled the familiar rusty old metal scent from when I was from the dungeons back then. I saw a movement near the door, which made me look up. There was the man that had kidnapped me the night before, but I couldn't see how he looked like since it was dark.

"I see that your finally awake then?" The man said, a menacing smile stretched out on his face.

"Oh and don't worry, you won't be seeing your little wolf soon," he said.

"W-what did you do?" I asked, still trying to reach out to my wolf.

"Just a little injection and 'poof' your wolf is gone," he chuckled.

I wanted to punch the man in the face, if only I wasn't chained up to the wall. What did he want from me anyway? I'm just a normal girl with a normal life. I didn't have enemies; not that I know of.

I curled up into a ball and went to the back of the prison, I was tired, I just wanted to go back to bed. I wish everything was a dream. But sadly, not all our 'wants' come true.

"I won't hurt you," the man promised. He moved closer to me, closer to where the light was. Emerald eyes stared back at me, I started fiddling with my fingers.

Gathering enough courage, I spoke. "What do you want from me?"

He ran a hand on his messy black hair. "I'm basically saving you but you should sleep for now," he patted my head and lifted a piece of cloth. He held it up my nose and I suddenly felt drowsy again. I fell asleep.

I woke up on a soft, dark bed. I don't remember being in here, the last thing I remember was those mesmerizing emerald green eyes. They were brighter than anything I had known of.

The door opened and in came the man that had kidnapped me. "Are you feeling better?" He asked.

Seriously?

"You kidnapped me and your asking me if I'm feeling better?" I growled at him.

"You were shivering when you were in my basement, I let you sleep in my bed and this is how I'm being repaid?" His voice rose at the last word.

"Yeah right. I'm so, so grateful you kidnapped me," I said in a mocking tone.

Even though I was very scared, I tried not to show it. I didn't want this guy to know I was scared of him.

He growled at me. "Just rest I'll come back later."

The moment he left the room, I immediately started looking around the room for an escape route, but no matter how much I looked, I can't find one.

It's been hours and I was just sitting here, in bed, trying to figure out how I could escape. The man who kidnapped me already gave me food to eat, but no, I couldn't risk getting poisoned and so I chose to starve.

The door opened and the man came in. "Have you seriously not eaten? I can't let you starve to death," he said.

"I can't die because of poison either."

"I didn't poison that."

"How do I know that your not lying?"

He sighed and said, "Fine then, don't eat if you don't want to."

Then he walked towards the bed and sat down. He relaxed his head on the headboard and stretched.

"Umm, get out of my bed," I said.

"This is technically my bed in my room."

I stood from the bed and walked towards a beanbag chair. Then I relaxed on the large beanbag and just glared at him. "When will you let me go?"

"What do you mean?"

"When will you let me out of here?"

"Once the war is over." He adjusted himself to a comfortable position.

"There's a WHAT?!" I screeched.

"The war has just begun, I came to save you from it," he shrugged.

Chapter 13

I can't believe it, there's a war and I'm just sitting here in a beanbag chair, waiting for things to happen. I wanted to escape, but the man is on the bed, watching my every move. I'm not hoping for someone to save me, they already have much things in their hands, I don't want to add to it.

Since I'd be staying here for a while, I might as well try to be comfortable. Before I could move another step, the door burst open. The man looked up.

"Ah, you're finally here. Don't worry I took care of your mate," the man said.

"I'm perfectly capable of taking care of my own mate," Caine growled.

"I'm not saying you can't, but those vampires that are attacking those wolves are very powerful, some have some witch in them too."

"Your also a vampire, why aren't you helping them?"

I gasped, "Your a vampire?!" I'm the dumbest one of the three.

The man's gaze went on me, "Yes, wasn't it obvious?"

He's a blood sucking vampire the whole time and I didn't know?! I thought werewolves had some sort of ability so that they could tell humans and vampires apart. Oh I almost fo rgot... the guy did some sort of injection that made my wolf disappear from my head.

Then the man turned to look at Caine. "I'm not in their clan, why should I help them?"

"Because your all vampires," Caine replied.

"Not all of us are that bad."

"C'mon, I just saved your mate from the war and this is how I'm being repaid?!" The man glared at Caine as he stood from the bed.

I just stared at the two of them as the drama unfolded. It's like a real movie, all that's missing is the popcorn. Just thinking of popcorn made me drool. I hadn't eaten for some time now. I looked at the table, there were still three more chocolate bars and a bag of candies. I ripped the plastic pack of the candies and started munching on the candies, while watching the two of them.

I stretched my arms at the large beanbag chair and took a little nap.

"You bastard! Did you put poison on the candies?!" A famil-iar voice growled.

"No I didn't! Why is all the blame on me?!" Another voice hissed.

I blinked my eyes and sat up. I was back on the bed, Caine and the vampire man sat next to each other, staring at me.

"Uhhh," I muttered.

"Are you okay?" Caine asked.

Did they mistakenly thought I passed out? I was just sleeping-

"Uhh yeah," I replied. This was awkward. I sat up and that's when my wolf perked up.

Hi, human! I missed you so much! She squealed.

I missed you too? What did the injection thing do to you?

Made me fall unconscious for a while, at least I'm back! She giggled.

Yeah, welcome back!

Where are we?

Some vampire's lair.

Well, at least mate is here, that's all that matters to me!

I blinked.

Why are all of them staring at us?

They think I got poisoned—

Oof, let them think that, then we can get special treatment, my wolf snickered.

I smirked mentally at my wolf. Great idea!

I snuggled and curled myself up in the blanket. They both stared at me worriedly, I just blinked and stared back.

"She doesn't look like she's been poisoned," the vampire guy said as he reached out to touch my forehead. Before he got to touch it, Caine swatted his hand away.

"Don't touch her," Caine growled.

"I was just checki-"

"Your making excuses to touch her."

"No I'm not-"

"Stop denying it!"

Okay, these two have lost it—I don't really get why they fight a lot but it's quite entertaining to watch. Caine rested a hand on my forehead, checking my temperature. And for some reason, I didn't want him to pull his hand back. His touch was warm and gentle, and I found myself closing my eyes, just focusing on his touch.

"Her temperature is normal, maybe I overreacted a little," Caine murmured.

"Okay then, I only stayed to check if she was fine," the vampire guy said as he stood up.

Caine pulled me into lap and I snuggled closer to him by instinct. I watched as the vampire guy left the room. Caine held up a bar of chocolate to my face. "Here, it'll make you feel better."

I grabbed the chocolate bar and ate it hungrily. Caine watched me with amusement in his eyes, his hand flew up to my bottom lip and gently rubbed the chocolate on it. Whenever and whatever part of me he touched, I didn't want him to let go, I had to force myself to not grab his arm and make his hand stay in the same place.

That's because of the mate bond, my wolf explained. It makes you want to feel his touch no matter what, don't worry, he also feels it. And even if you try to not think about it, it still pops back up in your head.

Caine withdrew his hand from cheek which he had been caressing just a few moments ago. He cuddled me tightly to his chest. I could hear his heart beating and it just made me feel more relaxed.

"I'm glad Daniel got you in here, the war... it's not going too well for us," Caine muttered. "And those half witch vampires have created a barrier so that the wolves within the place couldn't escape."

"Oh," was all I could get out.

I was sitting here in Caine's lap, safe, while the others were fighting to just survive. I want to help, but even if I wanted to, I couldn't. I had only been a wolf for a few days. I'm not trained-and I'm not brave enough to just go in a fight without knowing any moves.

Chapter 14

S weat poured from all over my face. "Come on, your hitting nothing but air," Caine's voice yelled. I took in a deep breath.

Yes, I tried training, which was a really bad idea. I couldn't even punch Caine without accidentally tripping from the force I was putting. And even though Caine was obviously going easy on me, I'm still screwed up.

"Okay, never mind this isn't working, just run around this area for now then?" It sounded more like a question than a statement, the other time he made me run around the area, it took me 37 minutes and 52 seconds. And my excuse was because 'I wasn't in the mood to run,' which was partly true, but the main reason I was so slow was because I never had a reason to run before and so I was never that fast.

I started running around the area, I wiped my sweat with a towel that I got in case I'd get sweaty and I looked like I had gotten a shower without drying myself right now.

I thought when I turned into a wolf I would be way faster and way stronger, but it seems like it hasn't took any effect. Or maybe I should actually make some effort and train before it takes effect? I don't really know.

I ran and ran for what seemed to be eternity, until I finally reached where Caine was standing. He looked bored.

Of course he would look bored, how long have you ran? An hour? Two? More?

I'm basically you and your basically me, so we're both slow at—

"Your back, earlier than I thought you would," Caine said. Earlier than he thought I would? Maybe it was a few seconds less from before, maybe?

Caine checked the stopwatch. "23 minutes and 17 seconds, much better than before. That's a really good improvement."

He didn't look like he meant it was a really good improvement for a wolf. Wolves are supposed to run much much more faster than that, but then again I'm new to these so he could give me an exemption?

Days had passed and I was getting better at the whole 'training' thing. The vampire's from this clan were sending a few men to help the wolves escape, little by little. Only the vampires could get in the barrier, and so no matter how hard Caine had tried to get in, he just couldn't, but the vampires can get in effortlessly.

I was worried for the other wolves that were fighting for their lives in there. Though I hadn't been close with wolves much, I still feel bad for them. Daniel and I had been getting along quite well on these few days, but Caine gets jealous each time I even just talk to him. But I get it, Alpha's are way more protective than a normal wolf.

I had read a lot about vampires and wolves during my free time, mostly to know more about their species, and to kill time. I was bored out of my mind whenever my 'training' was finished. Right now, I'm just sitting the side of my bed, drinking orange juice.

Suddenly, I choked. But before whatever the 'thing' in my orange juice could get into my throat, I spat it out. A seed. A freaking seed. I thought they were meant to put all the seeds out after they squeeze the oranges.

I suddenly felt dizzy, without knowing, I fell.

Good thing the bed caught me.

Black spots filled my vision as I tried to regain consciousness, but I blacked out soon after. I passed out.

"Who drugged her?! Who prepared the orange juice?" I heard a voice. That was obviously Caine's voice, I know it too well, but this time, it wasn't the soft, gentle Caine, it was the raging, furious one.

The men on the corner of the room shuffled their feet and fiddled on their fingers nervously. "Well? If none of you speaks up I'll just check the CCTV's and find out," another voice, that I assumed was Daniel's, spoke. He was much calmer than Caine was, but I could still hear a strain of disappointment and anger in his voice.

"We couldn't just assume— I mean without proof-," the man speaking struggled to find words, he was visibly trembling and his voice cracked as he spoke.

"Aren't the CCTV's enough proof? I'll check on it once she wakes up," Daniel said, a low growl erupting on the back of his throat.

I felt someone sit right next to where I was laying. Someone rested their hand on my forehead, checking my temperature. His hand sent sparks and shivers down my spine, the only person that had that effect on me was Caine. "She's definitely better than a while ago, her temperature was burning like fire just a few minutes ago but now it's cold... honestly it feels too cold," he muttered to himself.

I think burning like fire was better than being ice cold. Having a warm temperature means your alive, so it's definitely better. I think. Maybe.

Finally, I was able to open my eyes. The first thing I saw was Caine's comforting blue eyes, looking down at me. "Are you alright?" He asked.

"Mhm," I replied, still feeling dizzy. It wasn't completely a lie.

"Okay, you'll be here for a few hours to rest, since wolves heal much faster than humans." Then, Caine and Daniel both left the room, the men following them like lost puppies.

I clutched my stomach in pain. I got up from the bed and opened the curtain to reveal the window. I looked up the evening sky, it was a beautiful sight. But after a few moments of silence, the window crashed. The glass shards from the window pricked my skin and I cried in pain as blood oozed out of the pricks. A man stepped in the room and knocked me out.

Everything turned black, and I fell right into the vampire's awaiting arms.

Chapter 15

Dark, thunderous clouds filled the sky. The ground below was dry and unhealthy. Caine was still trying to get through the barrier. "Don't waste your energy, only vampires can get in the barrier," Daniel said to Caine. Caine tried to get in once more, running towards it with all his might. But in the end, he always kept being knocked back, always being sent flying away from the barrier, the same goes for who tries to get out of the barrier.

"I have to, my brothers... I can feel their pain, they are getting tortured!" Caine said, his voice laced with fury. He banged furiously on the invisible barrier.

"I tried getting them out before, they noticed immediately, they are the most guarded ones," Daniel said in an apologetic tone.

Caine sighed, he was obviously frustrated. "I will try to get through this barrier even if it would cost my life!" He cared about his brothers, as much as he cared for himself and his mate. They were bonded for years, they spent centuries together.

"Then what would your mate do without you? If you die, she won't have her other half," Daniel tried to reason. He cared for Sylvia, but he couldn't have her; she had a mate. He wanted the best for her, and if that meant keeping Caine alive, so be it. He blocked Caine from trying to get into the barrier, and knocked him out.

It was for his own good. He wouldn't survive in there.

I woke up from my dream and found myself in a cold and rusty basement. I knew too well that I was caged up again, and the bars were made of silver, it hadn't mattered when she was a human, but now that she was a wolf, it did.

I reached out and was about to touch the silver bar when my wolf screeched in my head.

Wait! Stop! Don't touch the silver, it will weaken me! My wolf screeched.

Okay, okay, I won't. Any ideas on how to escape? I asked.

Not really, the back of the wall... the back of the solid wall I mean, it's filled with silver. It will hurt a lot if we even try to escape...

I sighed, I needed to get out of this, I just need to figure out how. I looked around me and tried to search for any ways possible to escape. I lifted my hand and collapsed on the side of the wall. I couldn't really figure out to escape, not without hurting my wolf.

Eyyy, eyy! Don't go too close to the wall! My back hurts, aww awww!

I scooted away from all of the walls, which made me sit in the middle of the small, rusty, smelly room. Which made complete and perfect sense because it was technically a basement, and basements were supposed to be all creepy with spiders and cobwebs.

The door creaked open, revealing a young man with black hair and light brown eyes. He looked at her and smiled, no, not the nice, genuine smile that your friends give you. It was a cruel, menacing smile, almost one to say 'Hi, are you ready to die?'.

He stared at me, but I kept my eyes on the ground, knowing to not look a vampire in the eye. He snorted, "I guess you not as dumb as I thought you were."

"I'll take it as a compliment, thanks." I muttered bitterly.

"I won't hurt you if you tell me how that little Alpha and the other vampire groupie are doing to get some of the wolves out," he said with a snarl.

"I won't say a thing."

"Don't make me go the hard way. Though I'd really enjoy ripping you from limb to limb and munch you down to pieces, then drink that delicious smelling blood of yours, I need to know what you know."

I stayed silent, and allowed him to roam around the room while staring at me, wanting eye contact, but I wasn't going to give him that. "Tell me or I'll torture you with silver, I can chain you down and whip you until you spill out what you know, either way, you'd tell me everything," he growled.

My wolf whimpered in my head at the thought of being tortured with silver. My wolf wasn't immune to it, unlike how Caine and his brothers were. Suddenly, an idea struck my mind.

The freaky messaging or call thing that the wolves do through our heads!

Just before I could contact Caine, a frantic voice that sounded like Caine's echoed in my head.

Where are you? We just found out that you were away from your room and your scent smelled like you've left for a few hours now.

So I sent back, I don't know where I am but some vampire guy got me in his basement.

Shit, then I guess your in the barrier. Are you alright?

I'm fine, for now.

What do you mean for now?!

I don't know? Later, he'll probably torture me with silver or something.

You sound as if it's a joke, no, it's not a joke. You don't know how painful it is to have silver contact your skin, I felt it when I wasn't immune to silver yet. Your wolf will be pained a lot, and she will be out of your head to heal your wounds for quite some time; which leads to you being vulnerable, because without your wolf you won't have the extra strength, speed and transformation.

I know, I just—

Suddenly, our contact broke. I looked at the vampire towering over me, he threw his head back and laughed, just like how dramatic, cringey, evil villains do.

"Bro, this isn't a movie," I said, glaring at him. "You don't have to pretend to be some evil villain in a movie you know."

"It's just for the effects," he snarled. "Anyways, I was laughing about how your trying to contact your centuries-old alpha wolfie, who, apparently, hasn't grown a beard yet."

I glared at him, "And how old are you, leech?"

"Older than dirt. Anyways, that's besides the point, from now on, you won't be able to use that random phone thing in your mind. As long as your here."

Chapter 16

I was starved, beaten and poisoned during my two days captured in a basement. I don't know what will happen to me if this goes on. At least she gave her three meals a day, but she was still starved because they gave her very little amount of food whenever I was a 'bad girl' as the vampire liked to call it.

The door opened and the same vampire from her first day gave her a tray filled with food. I looked at him suspiciously at the sudden amount of food given. He just shrugged innocently and left the room without another word.

I sniffed the food and my wolf immediately said "Wolfsbane alert."

I sighed, no food for me I guess. I pushed the tray away from me and sat in the middle of the 'prison'. They had been weakening me and my wolf by silver and wolfsbane. And also by less food, or poisoned ones, which forced me not to eat.

The door creaked open, with some of the guards beside the vampire now. When he looked in my direction, he looked quite surprised at how I was still conscious, then his eyes flickered towards the tray which was still full. He sighed and shook his head. "I guess I underestimated your ability to sniff the wolfs-bane out, I should have..." his voice trailed away, remembering something and he quickly shut his mouth before he spilled more information.

They have held me captive mostly because I was the one to be able to lure Caine into this 'trap' of theirs. And that was when I started to hope that Caine wouldn't come to my rescue. I didn't want him in trouble just because I was. Even though I hadn't been with him for long, I cared for him.

The vampire looked at me then stared deep into my eyes. I tried to look away from his eyes, but I couldn't. Suddenly, I felt myself fall for his tricks, compulsion. He smiled at me devilishly.

"Who were the ones helping the wolves escape?"

I tried my hardest to restrain what he was asking me to do. I fought against it, tried my hardest to. "Sweetheart, it wouldn't exactly end too well for you if you keep trying to fight it," his deep velvety voice growled right at my ear.

I felt myself feel dizzier, and I started to lose consciousness but I was still sitting up, because of the vampire's outstretched arm, supporting me to keep my balance. Then I started rambling on without knowing or having control over what I was saying.

I was on a soft layer of material when I finally woke up and regained my consciousness and control of myself. I saw that I was no longer in the basement but in a small room with a soft, comfy bed in the middle of everything. A light yellow rug right below the bed. A desk with a chair pushed into the hollow space in the desk. Pale light lit the room, a light yellow curtain blocked the window from view, but it was thin enough to let sunlight pass through.

I sat up and walked over to the window. I opened the curtain and stared at the beautiful sky. This is my chance to escape. I saw no locks on the window to properly open it, so I grabbed the chair from it's place and crashed it to the window. Some of the glass shards pricked my skin, but that was my least concern right now, I heard faint thudding footsteps, which meant the vampires had already heard the crash.

I looked at the scenery down below. I would either land on a lake, bushes, grass, or mud. I just had to hope for a safe landing. Or I could try transforming to my wolf and land on my four paws, but it would cramp my bones once I turn back to my human form. I heard the footsteps grow louder by the second, I had to move quick. I jumped into the hole of the window and fell right into the lake, cold water rushed into my skin, leaving goosebumps. I tried to get up but realized that I couldn't. Something was holding onto my ankle. Huge, black tentacles wrapped itself around my waist, I tried to break free from it's hold, but it was too strong.

The beast took me down through the water, oxygen quickly running out of my lungs. If I don't move quick, I'll be doomed. With one last kick, I managed to break free from it's hold, but once I reached the surface of the water, I was met with vampires with angry eyes. One of them grabbed my arm and pulled me to the grass.

"Don't try to escape next time or we will give you a harsh punishment," one of them said, a low growl coming from the back of his throat.

One of the vampires grabbed me by my shoulders and was escorting me back to the building. This was my only chance to escape. I kicked him in the shin and ran away. I heard the vampires follow, running as fast as they could.

I rushed past the trees, going through zigzags to try and lure the vampires away from me. I have not dared to look back, but now I did. They were surprisingly fast at speed and was surprisingly close to me. There was no way they could lose track of me if I wouldn't be faster. So, with my last resort of strength, I ran even faster, hoping with all my might that the vampires would lose track of me.

I looked around and saw that the vampires were now gone, but I heard faint footsteps growing louder by every second, I had to leave, but just as I was about to start running again, my left foot started hurting, probably from the fall and the escape.

I heard the bushes make a soft ruffling sound, I tried to run but fell down to the ground. A shadowed figure went up to me. I closed my eyes, knowing I was doomed.

Chapter 17

A pair of hazel brown eyes stared at my shuddering figure. He held up a hand, and I thought he was going to punch me but then his hand gently caressed my hair. "What are you doing inside the barrier?" Daniel asked.

I was surprised that he was here, inside the barrier at the time I was in most need. "I was captured by the vampires," I whispered as if one of the vampires would hear me.

Then, Daniel did something that surprised me. He got a dagger out of his pocket then slid it to his wrist, blood dripping out of it. He held it near my mouth, which made me disgusted and I tried to turn away, but he grabbed my face and allowed the blood to drop into my mouth which I had to swallow.

"What was that for?" I said as I tasted the metallic taste of his blood.

"It was for you to leave the barrier, it's the only way," he explained as the wound in his wrist closed and healed on it's own.

"I need your blood to get through the barrier?!" I said in surprise.

"Mhm, it's the only way," was his response.

He led me towards the edge of the barrier and when I went out of it, I saw Caine leaning on a tree, looking stressed out. When he saw me, he immediately grabbed me and held me in a comforting embrace.

"I thought I lost you," he whispered as he put a strand of my hair in my ear. His chest was so warm and comforting, I wanted to be on it forever. I felt safe and secured in his arms, I didn't want to let go.

Daniel went towards us and said, "We should get out of here before the vampires do their 'checking up on the place' thing." Caine nodded and we left the area with a few other injured wolves.

When we reached the building, I saw a few vampires around the corner, whispering among themselves. Daniel immediately halted us to a stop. "Those aren't any of the vampires in my clan, it must be..." he trailed off, but that was enough for us to understand what he meant.

A sudden guilt crept up on me. I had been the one to tell those vampires everything about Daniel and his vampires, all that I knew anyway. But I had been the one to tell them all I knew once I had been...

Daniel's voice cut off through my thoughts. "They shouldn't know about us..."

"I think I told them about it when I was... under the vampire's control," I admitted. The guilt weighed off my shoulders ever so slightly, but the guilt that consumed me was still visible in y eyes.

"It's fine, you weren't in control of yourself, it isn't your fault," Daniel said, attempting to comfort me. He gently touched my shoulder, but earned a growl from Caine. His growl attracted the vampires and one of them snarled at our direction.

"Oops," Caine muttered.

The vampires started walking towards us, the black haired, red eyed vampire that was the one who took care- or should I say, tortured me, at the front, probably their 'leader'.

When they were close enough for us to hear what they were saying, the black haired, red eyed vampire said, "I see your back with your little friends then? At least I got enough information from you to know who are the ones responsible for escapees."

I heard some of the other vampires snicker, and I saw Caine's hands curl into fists.

"And I'm glad you and your little pathetic friends lead us to where your little hide out is," he said as he gestured towards the building. "We just had a head start when you all were slowed by those lame wolves."

I could literally feel Caine heating up, and as much as I wanted to punch the guy in the face, I didn't want Caine to hurt himself, so I wrapped my arms around his arm, hoping it would be enough to calm him down. It did calm him down, a little bit, because he started stroking my hair absent-mindedly. I was too distracted to notice that Daniel and the vampire was deep in discussion.

"Just stop minding my business with the wolves and I'll leave your group alone," the vampire growled.

"Elijah, I don't want to repeat myself," Daniel said firmly. By his tone and facial expression, anyone could tell that he was pissed.

"Are you really willing to sacrifice your group's vampires just to save these wolves? They have stomped over us for years! This is our time to take revenge on those ignorant, little wolves," Elijah said, crossing his arms over his chest.

"Didn't our overall master sign an agreement to have peace with the wolves? Your breaking the rules, I won't be surprised if you were to be banished," Daniel countered. Elijah obviously cringed at what he had said.

If there is an overall leader for the vampires, then who is the overall leader of the wolves? I asked my wolf out of curiosity.

Caine and his brothers, also called 'The Cadell Brothers', my wolf said helpfully.

My jaw almost dropped open and fell to the ground.

Say what?!

Yes, dumbhead, our mate is one of the overall leaders, isn't he cute?

Overall leaders? I echoed, I shook my head when I realized how dumb I sounded.

Yes, there are more Alpha's, but of course, Caine is the hottest-

I'm not here to discuss about their looks, I mentally glared at my wolf.

Whatever, she mumbled, mentally returning my glare.

I had been so consumed in thought and talking to my wolf that I hadn't noticed that Daniel and Elijah were shooting each other death glares. Both of their fists were clenched, and I was afraid that both of them would throw themselves to each other and attack. I felt Caine gently caressing my back, comforting me.

Chapter 18

Something that Daniel had said got Elijah so mad that he lunged at him. I cringed when I saw blood dripping out of the wound that Daniel had, but luckily, vampires couldn't suffer blood loss. I felt Caine tugging me away from the fight, but the other vampires lunged at us. We fought the vampires, but we were outnumbered.

Vampires poured out of the building, as soon as Elijah saw he and his companions were outnumbered and surrounded, he nodded towards his group. He looked at us and said, "We'll meet again." Then, with a flick of his wrist, they all disappeared, leaving purplish smoke.

"Stupid hybrids," Daniel growled.

We went back to the building and we all went to the clinic, almost all of us were injured. I wasn't injured that much but I still wanted to be checked up on. I had to be carried there by Caine, since my leg wouldn't work itself. And it had to be Caine because he was the only one not injured, but even if there was someone else, Caine wouldn't let them.

Eeek, that was the best experience ever!

I mentally rolled my eyes at my wolf.

I went into the room they told me to, a doctor went in after me, then started doing what the others did, but not before giving me a smug smile. The wounds on my leg that was left by the tentacles of the monster in the lake swelled up even more as he rubbed an unknown substance into it. I felt the pain go worse, as he rubbed a piece of cloth on it.

After a few seconds, I felt unbearable pain right at where my wounds were, I blacked out.

"We can't trust anyone anymore, the vampire that treated her is a traitor," I heard Caine growl at Daniel, smacking his hands on the desk in front of him. The desk swayed violently, about to fall. If Caine had done it any harder, it would be in pieces by now.

I shifted my position in the bed. When Caine saw me move, he immediately stood up and sat by my side. I opened my eyes and stared at his piercing blue eyes filled with worry and concern.

"What happened?" I asked.

Daniel and Caine both looked at each other, they were silent for a while, until Daniel spoke up. "The doctor treating you was on the other vampire's side, a spy. And he didn't do anything to help your wounds, actually it's quite the opposite, and now we tried questioning him but he won't say anything besides 'I was supposed to bring Sylvia back to them,' which was already obvious, anyways, we killed him when he wouldn't reveal anything else."

I winced at the thought of the guy bleeding out, dying. Even though he wanted to take me back to that evil vampire's lair, I kind of felt bad for him. Kind of.

He deserved it, my wolf said smugly, she was, after all, the one who helped me heal from the substance that the guy put on my wounds.

I was so lost in thought that I didn't notice Caine growling and saying things that made the men that had just entered cringe. Daniel stopped him from lunging onto the men, "They weren't the one who wrote the letter, they just found it."

Caine struggled against his grip, he ended up making Daniel fall towards the men, then the men fell towards different parts of the room, crashing and breaking things. I jumped up from my bed and dodged a vase falling from the upper shelf right on top of me. Caine stood in the middle of all the mess, seemingly to be unaffected by all the trouble he had caused.

When the men finally got hold pf themselves, they glared at Caine and held eye contact, which was a sign of disrespect. He was about to slap one of them when Daniel held up a hand. "They don't know wolf customs and tradition."

Even with what Daniel had said, I felt my wolf wanting to take control and lunge at the man, feeling my wolf's fury on how our mate got disrespected, but I just pushed her back, not having enough energy to even walk back to my bed. I limped my way back and slumped onto the bed.

"Let's take this outside," Daniel growled, still watching Caine's every movement in case he decided to cause trouble again. They all went out of the room, leaving me alone.

I'm guessing that whatever they were about to talk about was something they didn't want me to hear, or I wasn't supposed to hear, it didn't matter either way. With my wolf's hearing, I was able to overhear some words like 'threat', 'dumb mutts' and others that wasn't really useful nor making any sense.

The door opened and I saw Caine holding out a piece of paper, he held it out to me. I got the crumpled letter in my hands and straightened it. The words were cramped because of the force of being crumpled, but the handwriting was neat.

The letter read:

Dearest Alpha,

I would watch my back if I were you, just a fair warning, just because you caught my worker at the last minute of your mate being kidnapped doesn't mean we are all as reckless as he was to allow the girl to scream. Yes, you don't have much weaknesses, but upon my spy's observation, your mate is clearly one of them, and she's the reason you'll be taken down. I don't understand why the vampire, Daniel, would help such pathetic werewolves such as yourself, but whatever reason that may be, I do not care; I will kill him with the rest if he would continue to help you and your pack. I hope you sleep well, and enjoy your time with your mate while she lasts.

Toodles ⊠,

Elijah

Chapter 19

I felt my breath quicken at each word I read. Someone was threatening Caine, using me. Obviously, being his mate, I would be one of his strongest weaknesses that his enemies could use against him since, basically, I was his 'other half'.

After reading the threat letter, I put it on Caine's outstretched palm. As soon as the paper made contact with his skin, he clenched his hand, causing the paper to crumple up again.

"There are more traitors in the pack and in your coven," Caine said as he threw the crumpled piece of paper towards the desk. "How else would he be able to put this letter in your grounds if you doubled up the security!? How can we trust anyone now?!"

Daniel seemed to be at loss for words, he trusted his coven but he knew what Caine was saying was true. He put his hands on the sides of his head. "But who could possibly be the ones to betray us? Betray the coven? Betray me? Betrayal is straight execution, that's the rule of our coven, who would even risk their own lives for those people who they barely know?!"

"Unless he offered protection or is threatening him," Caine answered. Daniel started pacing around the room. That was the last thing I saw until I fell asleep.

I woke up in the morning, smelling the delicious scent of pancakes. I looked around me, I wasn't in the same room as before, I was in a much more spacious room, and I seemed to be at a higher part of the building. I saw huge black wings attached onto a man fly by, near the window. I almost screamed but caught myself in time. If he was here to kidnap me, I should not scream or else he'd find me easily.

I sat up and saw a note on my bedside table. I picked it up and read the note.

The note read:

Good morning, sunshine! Since the incident happened the night we saved you, we realized it is no longer safe for any of us to go anywhere without security. I've doubled up the security around the building, and put vampires stationing around your room. As for your window, there are vampires flying around to patrol around your window, just in case.

-Daniel

I smiled, even though he hadn't known me for long, he already cared for me, and I was vey grateful for that. I looked around the room. It was just the same room I had with Trix before, now that I think about it, I really missed her. What had happened to her and my best friends? Were they alright? I sighed as I went into the bathroom built in the room.

I took a shower, changed into decent clothes and went downstairs. I cringed at the creaking sound of the stairs. I smelt the delicious scent of pancakes grow nearer as I approached the kitchen. I saw a few women dressed in an old fashioned maid outfit work inside. I approached the plate of pancakes but a lady that seemed to be in her 50's stopped me.

"Those are for someone else, I could make you some if you'd like though," she said with a smile. "Oh and the name's Eliza. Short for Elizabeth."

I smiled at her hospitality, "My name's Sylvia, and sure I'd like some if you don't mind."

She nodded and started making pancakes on the counter. Just like how my mom used to...

Flashback:

"Mommy! Do I smell.. PANCAKES?!" Little Sylvia squealed. She ran over to her mom, making her mother fall face first towards the pancake syrup.

"Be patient, Sylvia, or no pancakes for you!" My mother said, patting my head. "And, uhh, we're short on pancake syrup now that more than half of it spilled."

"PANCAKE!!!" My little brother screamed from upstairs. He ran down the stairs, holding his teddy bear on one hand while waving the other.

We used to love pancakes at home, since it was unusual for us to get a decent meal during breakfast, our parents usually save the rest of our food for lunch and dinner. We, humans, don't have much, because we were hiding from the wolves to live in freedom.

My little brother and I helped my mother make the pancakes, laughing and talking all the while.

End of Flashback

A tear fell down my cheek. I missed those times with my family, though we were hiding from the werewolves, we still had some of our fun and happy moments. But now I don't even know if they were alive.

"Are you okay?" I heard Elizabeth ask beside me, holding out a plate of pancakes.

"Yeah, it's nothing," I answered, my voice cracked and that proved that I wasn't okay. I got the fork and started eating, I noticed that most of the other girls have left the kitchen and were taking their breaks.

I looked at Elizabeth, "Aren't you going to take your break as well?" I asked.

She shook her head, "At least one of us are supposed to keep someone company if there's someone in the kitchen, I'm here to assist you."

"You can eat with me, I can't finish six pancakes on my own anyway," I said as I sat down and patted the seat next to me.

"I can't eat with you, even if I wanted to, I'm just a slave here, it's disrespectful."

"I'm not one of those bossy leaders, c'mon," I urged.

"Did you just call me bossy?!" I heard Daniel say at the doorway. He had a childish pout on his lips. He crossed his arms around his chest and pretended to be offended.

Elizabeth immediately apologized to him while bowing, but I just rolled my eyes.

Daniel sat beside me and started eating the pancakes on his plate. He finished all eight of them. I didn't notice vampires had such a big appetite. I started eating too, but was too full to eat any more than two pancakes.

"Why are you two eating without me?" I heard Caine's voice on the doorway.

Chapter 20

I was walking down the hallway to my room when I suddenly heard Caine and Daniel yelling at each other. I pressed my ear towards the wooden door to hear what they were saying.

"I can't just lay around, my pack is in danger! If my brothers and I are captured, the other packs that we rule will also be in danger!" I heard Caine growl after what he had said.

"Well, my clan is also as important as the safety of the wolves, I can't just start a random war!" Daniel's voice was laced with anger.

I started walking away, knowing I knew enough when Caine suddenly said, "I can smell your scent."

I froze. I am so screwed. I opened the door and went in awkwardly. Caine patted the seat right next to him, gesturing for me to sit down. I sat beside him, the chair softly creaking as I plopped down onto it.

There was an awkward silence until Daniel decided to break it.

"Why were you eavesdropping?" He asked.

"Just curious," I mumbled, fiddling with my fingers nervously.

"If you were anyone else, I would've had your memory erased..." he started. Having your memory erased was very painful, it would give you daily headaches after the person has erased your memory, but the person who cast it would also be weaker than usual for a few days.

I stood up to leave the room, before he changed his mind, but a warm hand caught my wrist. I groaned, did he change his mind about not punishing me now?

"Don't eavesdrop next time, these are matters to be discussed by us only," I heard Daniel say from behind me. I didn't look back, I just went straight to the door and out of the room.

When I heard the door click behind me, I went into my room and started pacing around, trying to figure out what they meant. When will they stop hiding secrets from me?

I sat on my bed, reading random books on my bedside table that were for the guests, since this was one of the guest rooms they put me in. It was all about vampires, witches, and wolves. I wonder if there were more magical species, most mythical and supernatural creatures usually hide from other kinds to avoid getting hunted down, which made me even more curious.

I put the last book down, I have read all four of the books placed on the table. Now I didn't know what to do. Was there a library here somewhere? I was really curious about other supernatural creatures. I wanted to know more.

I stood up and twisted the doorknob, opening the door. I ran past the hallway, then got lost. I forgot about my bad sense of direction. I saw a shadow walk past me, I immediately looked around by instinct. When the figure was close to touching me, I dodged and threw a punch right on the man's face. I heard a soft grunt, he was stunned, he didn't expect me to react that way. I took the opportunity to open the lights to the hallway.

A man stood, covering the part of his face that I had punched. He had fangs that rested on his lower lip. He wore a white T-shirt and jeans, which surprised me because I actually thought vampires actually wore robes and hideous things like the TV.

"Sorry, I thought I was being attacked or something," I said as I looked at the punch's results. It was really red, it was going to bruise soon, but to my surprise, it healed in a blink of an eye.

"No, actually, if you didn't stop me I would have attacked you, we, vampires hate werewolf blood, but your only half-blood, and it's been a while since I tasted fresh human or half-human blood."

Okay, now I kind of wish that I was born a pure-blooded wolf, just so that I wouldn't get daily attacks from hungry vampires. I probably look like a walking blood bank to this vampire right now.

I just stared at him as he got a blood bag from his pocket and drank from it hungrily. He finished the whole thing in less than a minute. Wow, he really must be hungry. He looked up and was surprised when he still saw me there.

"Do you need something? Because if you don't I suggest going as far as you can from me, it's very tempting to drink your blood you know," he said as he pointed to the blood bag that was now empty. Was that a threat? That my blood would soon be sucked dry like how he did to the blood bag?

"Uhhh, can you help me find the library?" I asked. "Preferably before you become more thirsty and suck me dry," I added. He grinned and led the way.

After a few minutes, he started clutching his head while walking. When I looked at his eyes, they were flashing from red to their normal light brown color every second. He came to an abrupt stop and grabbed another blood bag from his pocket and gulped it down. His eyes stopped flashing and he started walking normally again.

"I forgot to ask, what's your name?" I asked.

"Lucas, yours?" He replied.

"Sylvia."

We reached a door with a wooden sign, the word 'Library' was written on it in cursive letters. He held the door open for me. I thanked him and went inside. I heard the door close with a loud 'click'. I started looking through cover to cover, until I finally found what I had been curious about since before.

The title read:

The Pure-Blooded Wolves.

Chapter 21

Purebloods are now very rare as most of the werewolves alive are either half-bloods or hybrids. When a human is turned by a pure-blooded wolf, the human turned into a werewolf is still a half-blood but they will still inherit a little bit of the purebloods' abilities.

Since the purebloods are very rare and are close to extinction, purebloods try to keep their family line pure. Because of this, married couples arrange their children's marriage to keep the family's blood pure. The effect of these arranged marriages was that the couple usually doesn't love each other, they just treat each other as strangers, but when in front of their parents, they pretend to have affection for each other. Because of these arranged marriages, they were forced to leave their mates and reject them if they weren't purebloods. What the parents didn't notice was that some of their children committed suicide because of the loss of their mates, because it was too depressing. Some arranged couples are lucky enough to develop feelings for each other, or when the other person is their mate.

Pureblooded children's childhood isn't as lively as a normal wolf's. Purebloods are constantly being hunted down by hunters, vampires, witches, and other supernatural and mythical creatures. A pureblooded child's childhood is filled with training on how to use their abilities and how to use self-defense in case they get kidnapped.

Witches are usually the ones who hunt purebloods down. They start with the children or the newborns because they are the easiest to catch. They grow the newborns and the children until their powers fully develop, they feed, train and take care of them properly until their powers reach their peak. When their powers have fully developed, the witches suck the power out of them, leaving them powerless. Sometimes, they leave them to the werewolves, or they make them slaves to serve themselves.

Vampires hunt down the purebloods to make them as their warriors or soldiers. Vampires despise wolves a lot, but due to the contract the Lord of Vampires has signed, they could not just start a war just like that. But what the wolves didn't notice was that there were many flaws in the contract they had signed. The purebloods that were captured by the vampires are usually kids (5-12 years old) and take good care of them until they turn into teenagers, after that, it's all non-stop training every day, only Sunday as their rest day. They make these purebloods they have captured into believing that the other wolves are evil and want them dead, they tell all the lies they could think of, to make these wolves hate their own kind.

These pureblooded wolves are so pitiful, I thought. When I was about to flip the page, a sound from right outside my door alarmed me. I was debating whether or not to check outside or stay inside when the door burst open, revealing a very hungry vampire.

His black hair was messy, his eyes were bright red in color, it was glowing. He smirked when he found me. "No one told me there was a half-blood in here, God, I'm so hungry," he said as he licked his lips.

"Can't you just drink from your blood bag or something?" I asked as gently as possible.

"Yeah but you look like a walking blood bag in my eyes." And in a blink of an eye, he was in front of me. He grabbed the back of my neck and pulled me closer. My neck was bare, giving him more access to it. I screamed as he sunk his fangs into my neck. I suddenly felt dizzy, my vision blurring, my body went limp, and fell to the ground. Soon, I passed out.

When I woke up, I was still on the ground. I touched the part of my neck that he had bitten on, it stung when I touched it. When I withdrew my hand, dry blood filled my finger that I used to touch my neck.

I found a random first aid kit on a table nearby. I grabbed it and unzipped the zipper, I started cleaning my wound, after

I did, I went over to one of the mirrors that surrounded the grand library. I was surprised to see that there were no bite marks on my neck. There wasn't any mark or wound on it, it was as if he hadn't even bitten me.

Then it clicked in my mind.

I was a werewolf now, half-werewolf at least, and one of the advantages was being able to heal quicker than normal humans do. I guess I don't actually need the first aid kit.

I packed the first aid kit back in place, zipped it, and placed it back to where it was. I looked at the large window the library had, I didn't notice that it was already late afternoon. I opened the door and went straight to the kitchen, I am so hungry.

When the maids working there saw me, their eyes widened. "Master has been looking everywhere for you!" One of them exclaimed.

Master? As in Daniel? Usually, Caine was the one to go look for me...

"Uhh I was in the library and-" I was interrupted when someone hugged me from the back.

"I thought you got kidnapped again!" Daniel laughed. "I don't know where Caine is, I think he was looking for you too, I'll go find him so that-" His eyes suddenly widened. "Why do you smell like- dry blood?" he asked.

"I was uhh- attacked by a random vampire?"

"Who?" His voice seemed calm, but his eyes started flashing from red, black, and green. His fists started clenching and unclenching.

"I don't know-"

"You don't know who attacked you?!" He asked. He slapped his hand on his head. "Then how am I supposed to know who did it out of all the vampires in this place?"

"It was me," a voice said from behind him.

Chapter 22

- -

"I just took some sips- it wasn't that much," the man that had attacked me said.

"Jake, she's never been bitten before, it would hurt more since she isn't used to it. Didn't we provide all the vampires in this building enough blood bags each day?! You can't just go attack random people like that!" Daniel growled at him.

"Uhh, where is Caine?" I asked, interrupting their very heated conversation. Both their head snapped in my direction.

"I don't know, he was looking for you when we were also searching for you but I don't know where he is right now," Daniel answered, still glaring daggers at Jake.

I searched around the whole building until I reached a weird-looking stone door. I pushed it, but it wouldn't budge. I pushed harder, and this time, it opened a little bit. I looked at the small opening I had made. The door leads to a creepy-looking basement, and when I looked at it from the side, I noticed another door, but it was wooden.

My curiosity got the best of me and I pushed even harder at the stone door, when it only opened a little, I leaned my whole body towards it and pushed with all my might. When it finally opened, I stumbled a little from leaning too hard on the stone door.

I walked into the room, and if I was going to be honest, the room looked really old. I walked towards the wooden door, and when I was just about to open it, I heard footsteps from the other side.

My eyes went wide when the door burst open, and when Elijah came out of it, with two other vampires behind him. I took a step back when I realized they were armed.

When Elijah first noticed me, he smirked. "Is the little princess trying to save their mate?" he taunted. He walked closer to me as I backed away, his boots clinking on the wooden floor. I stopped walking backward when I realized it was a dead end. Elijah laughed humorlessly.

"YOU-! Did you-" I started, not knowing what to say.

"Well, whenever you get in danger, Caine or Daniel always saves you, but what if they were the one in danger? Would you be able to save them?"

I felt a sting hit me when he said those words. But what could I say? He was sort of right. Whenever I got in trouble, Caine or Daniel were always there for me, because I was weaker than they are and they always try to protect me. But what about me?

I couldn't save them, or at least I don't think I could. He smiled at me when he realized how his words had affected me.

Elijah signaled the two vampires to stop blocking the doorway. When they stepped out, my eyes widened when I saw Caine chained down on the wall, bleeding. Elijah went closer to me, and he spoke near my ear. "You two clearly aren't a good fit. But since you tried to rescue your little mate, I'll let you have him... but mark my words, I'll come back. And when I do, I won't show any mercy."

He allowed me to enter the room, and I immediately ran to Caine, checking his wounds and injuries. I looked back at Elijah, and when we made eye contact, the words 'I'll come back, and I won't show any mercy', went into my mind, as if he were speaking into it. Without a word, he and his companions disappeared in a puff of purple smoke.

Cool disappearing act, I must say.

"Are you okay?" I asked Caine.

He nodded weakly, but I could tell by his appearance that he wasn't okay. He had blood all over his clothing, and he seemed to lack energy. I tried pulling the silver chains off, but ended up getting my hand burned. My burn on my arm didn't hurt as much as pure-blooded wolves did though, because I was just a half-blood. "Use.. gloves," he managed to murmur before slipping out of consciousness.

I looked around the place, I knew that Elijah must have left the key somewhere in here. I saw a brown paper bag and looked into it. Inside was a silver key, why did everything have to be silver when werewolves were kind of allergic to silver?!

Caine's advice drifted into my head, like a replaying radio. 'Use gloves'. I don't have time to look for gloves so I ripped a huge portion from the paper bag and used it to be my 'glove'. I unlocked the chains that were used to hold Caine captive.

How the hell was I supposed to bring him back? He's way too heavy-

Or I could just wait until he wakes up.

I waited a whole hour just to wait for him to wake up, and when he did, I allowed him to rest for a while before leading us out of the place. He was limping a little and slightly leaned towards me whenever he would lose balance.

"I thought werewolves heal fast." I wondered out loud.

"Mhm, we do, but I'm too weak to heal right now," he muttered as he tested his arm, waving it around. He flinched when his shoulder started aching.

"You shouldn't move around- the pain will worsen."

"I savor the pain, I'm used to it," he smiled and added, "No need to feel bad."

I still felt bad.

When we finally reached the staircase which led to the living room, my legs felt numb. Why did they have to have such a big place anyway? I looked at Caine. He didn't seem bothered by how long we had been walking and climbing stairs, instead, he was flexing his bicep, again and again. When he caught me staring, I immediately looked away, my cheeks turning a little pinkish.

"Don't worry, it's perfectly normal to be attracted to my charms," he said with a grin. I playfully smacked his chest.

"Hmph!"

Daniel was seated among the people in the living room, watching TV. I guess they didn't really notice our disappearance, since we did disappear together, they might have thought we just wanted some alone time. But when Daniel's neck snapped toward our direction, he gasped when he saw how bloody Caine looked.

Chapter 23

"Hold up a sec. You're telling me that Elijah got past our guards and held Caine hostage in my own freaking house?!" Daniel asked, pronouncing the last four words much more. He started pacing around.

"I literally doubled up security and this happened?!" He said, talking to himself more than to anyone else.

I understood why he was so frustrated, knowing he put so much effort so that no one else would be kidnapped again. "Don't blame yourself for what happened, it's no one's fault." I said as gently as possible.

He sent me a weak smile. "You should go to bed while Caine's in the infirmary. I think you deserve a good night's rest."

I smiled and wished him a good night.

Elijah laughed humorlessly as he mercilessly slashed another wound on Caine's arm. He seemed to be enjoying torturing people.

"You always save your mate, but will she be able to save you?" Elijah said as he licked the blood dripping from the blade.

"I hate pure werewolf blood, but a blood of a royal really makes my day." He walked over to one of the other vampires who were watching him as they chuckle at how helpless Caine looked.

"Master, I am quite impressed of how you were able to lock him up so quickly, but a royal couldn't be taken down so fast, may I ask how?" One of the vampires asked.

"Quite? Your only quite impressed by the amount of magic I have conjured?!" Elijah boomed.

The vampire immediately cringed and said, "Master, I do not mean it like that, what I meant was-"

"Yes, yes, I already know what you meant. I will tell you how I was able to take down a royal very quickly since you all seem eager." Elijah replied.

"I simply have to temporarily lock his powers, though I'm afraid you lower-class hybrid can not use that much amount of magic before passing out. But before you do that, you have to weaken him, so that he won't be able to fight off the magic." Elijah explained.

Elijah went back to tormenting Caine. Each flinch he made made my heart break into pieces.

I woke up because of a loud scream, it still echoed through the walls of my bedroom then to the halls. It took me a while to realize that it was my own scream. The walls in the building were not soundproof so if anything happens, they will be alerted.

Lucas burst into the room, his eyes wandering around before zeroing on me. I had forgotten he was in a room right next to mine.

"Hey, are you okay?" He asked.

"Y-yeah, just had a nightmare, is all." I answered. "I hope I didn't disturb your sleep though."

He chuckled. "Vampires don't sleep, hon."

Oh.

I felt my cheeks flush in embarrassment. "Then I'm sorry for bothering whatever you were doing."

"Eh. I wasn't really doing anything so it's fine."

Just at that moment, vampires started hissing something I couldn't quite understand. But Lucas seemed to know what they meant and a look of horror filled his face.

"Is something wrong?" I asked him. Some vampires were running towards the room filled with weapons, so I assumed there was something bad going on.

"They broke in," Lucas answered as he grabbed me by the arm and led me towards the room of weapons. "Master ordered you to be in the basement, where the pregnant women, children, and newborn vampires are. But he also said he wanted you to be armed, just in case."

I blinked. "You know I'm not pregnant, right?"

He chuckled weakly. "Yeah. But master ordered so... unless I want to be shouted at in my own brain I'd do it."

"What's going on anyway? Let me guess, Elijah?" I asked

"Hmm? Yeah, he wanted payback for us bugging in their business."

He gave me a gun and left me in the basement along with the pregnant women, children, and newborn vampires. The newborns were locked in chains because their bloodthirst was uncontrollable. When I first came in, they thrashed around the locks, trying to break free to drink my blood. The children were more mature than the newborns who were just turned though they were older when it comes to bloodthirst, the children were better at controlling it.

I wasn't too happy about having to sit here and do nothing while the other vampires were fighting off whoever intruded. 'I'll come back, and I won't show any mercy'. Elijah's words echoed in my mind as if he was reminding me about it. Oh no. What if he was the one who intruded?

One of the soldiers named Oscar told us that the basement was hidden and no one else knew about it except the vampires living in this building.

I blinked hard at what he said. "Elijah was here with two vampires yesterday," I said. "So it isn't really top secret anymore."

Oscar looked at the other soldiers who seemed confused at what I had said. The soldier to his right spoke up. "You were probably just seeing things," he said in a firm voice.

Uhh hello?? Caine was brought back all bloody and bruised from the basement. Who do you think did it?

But I just kept my mouth shut because they were showing off their razor-sharp teeth at me. I heard footsteps coming from where the stone stairs were to be. The soldiers didn't seem alarmed, thinking it was one of the other soldiers, reporting back.

I grabbed my gun and made sure it was fully loaded, the soldiers looked at me in confusion. "It's just one of the others reporting back," one of them told me.

I ignored him, it was better to be prepared than to regret. I knew they sent a soldier up the stairs to check on what was happening upstairs, but just in case it was someone else, I couldn't take my chances.

The soldiers did a double-take at what they had seen.

Elijah held the bloody head of the soldier they had sent.

Chapter 24

I pointed my gun at Elijah but he didn't seem to care. He strode confidently towards the soldiers, easily blocking their attacks.

When Oscar and I made eye contact, I made a face that said, 'I told you so.' Elijah made an 'ok' signal to his back, and even more vampires came spilling into the basement, grabbing the innocent, helpless vampires. I shot as many vampires as I could, some of them dodged, some got stunned and some got injured. But none seemed to be dying, not even close.

The soldiers that were supposed to be protecting us were already slacking because they weren't prepared. It was their fault to ignore my warning. A vampire approached me from my back, but before I could shoot her with my gun, she managed to clip my hands on my back, letting the gun fall to the ground and allowing her to keep me hostage.

I wriggled against her grasp, but she was still stronger than I was. She tied me on a chair with a rope, then left me to discuss things with Elijah.

Wrong move, buddy.

My wolf helped me unleash my claws, and I used it to cut the ropes off of me. They didn't seem to notice that I was free, so I sneaked out of the basement. I looked up the stairs before going up. I saw 3 guards roaming around the exit. I couldn't take too long to escape, they'd notice I was gone and would look for me. But could I get through 3 guards, on my own?

If I couldn't defeat the female vampire that had taken me down easily, how could I take three male vampires down? I looked around me, finding for something, anything, to use against them.

I grabbed a random gun which was discarded at the bottom steps. I saw it was still loaded with some ammo. I only had five shots. I aimed the gun at the most muscular guy if ever I needed to choose between who I have to injure or kill first, it would be him.

I shot, but he moved away in time as if he had eyes at the back of his head. He looked around and pointed me out to the other two. I shot him again, this time, managing to injure his leg, which I had been aiming for so that he couldn't attack me. I did the same for the rest, aiming towards the hip and the other the thigh.

I ran past them as I heard raised voices coming from the basement. I passed through a couple of vampires, but I just dodged their attacks and ran away, making them lose track of me.

I heard voices from the main living room of the building. I weighed the chances of it being Daniel and his vampires or Elijah and his vampires. I wasn't really sure, but I opened the door anyway.

What lay inside took me by surprise. Both Daniel, Caine, and a few other vampires were all tied with ropes to a chair and a unique silver binding on each of their wrists, draining their energy.

Elijah was on a couch, talking casually to his friends as if this was just normal. I tried sneaking my way to the others but one of his friends pointed me out to him. I froze when his gaze turned to me. When he sat straighter, I watched his every move, I knew he would pounce on me any moment now. To my surprise, his shoulders relaxed again and he slumped onto the couch.

"Eh, you finally showed up. I knew you would try to save your matie, and probably the bloodsucker too," Elijah said, his friends snickered.

He smiled that sickening smile of his while I gulped when chains wrapped itself's around my body. I struggled against the chains' grip, but each time I moved, the tighter it gets. I stopped struggling once I realized if I would go on, the chains would choke me to death. So instead of struggling against the chains' grip, I took my time to glare daggers at the vampires sitting on the couch.

Elijah just picked up a teacup and sipped tea, then placed it back on the plate. "Don't waste your time staring at us, I mean, I know I'm gorgeous but that stare is kinda creepy."

How I wanted to kick that man square in the face-

My thoughts were interrupted when Elijah started coughing and wrapping his arms around his stomach. The female vampire who sat beside him roared, "WHO POISONED HIS DRINK?!"

I watched as the female vampire, who turned out to be his mate, went out of the room and came back a few minutes after with a glass cup filled with light green liquid. "Here, drink this. It'll cure you but it will leave some lingering effects," the female vampire said.

I never knew that someone as cruel as Elijah could have someone to care about him. Elijah's thumb grazed over the girl's cheek and he wiped a tear that escaped her eye. His other hand got the glass cup and he drank it in one gulp. "I- I don't know why a lot of our allies try to poison you," the female vampire sobbed.

Now I feel bad for them, it was obvious they cared a lot for each other.

My eyes drifted off to stare at Caine, involuntarily. My cheeks flushed when I found him staring at me too. I hastily looked away from him. I looked back at the couple, Elijah had drops of blood dripping out of his mouth. "It's because I have... many.. enemies," he said, pausing each word to gasp for air.

The female vampire looked around the room, to find something to heal her beloved. The rest of their friends had already left the room, they were obviously fake friends, they didn't care about Elijah nor did they care for the female vampire, they only cared about the status they have in their coven.

The girl's eyes landed on Caine, and she charged on him, shaking his shoulders as she said, "Wolves know more about healing, right? Please heal him, I'll do anything!" She said desperately.

Chapter 25

I t was like the whole room had paused. The female vampire looked at Caine desperately. Elijah blinked hard. "Selena, I can find a cure on my own, I don't need that dog's help," he said firmly.

Selena shook her head. "You have been like this for a few months, we don't know who's behind all the poisoning and you're growing weaker and weaker day by day." Her voice sounded weak. I looked at Selena, then at Elijah.

My brain started to process what was happening.

Selena and Elijah were like, opposites. Elijah was merciless, a bit heartless, and doesn't care about anything except Selena probably. Selena was gentle, caring, and considerate, so how in the world were they mates?!

Mates~, my wolf echoed in my head.

Caine looked at Selena then at Elijah, not knowing whether or not this was some sort of trickery.

"I know you probably don't believe me right now, but please help him," Selena said, grabbing a silver key with crooked ends from Elijah's pocket. Elijah immediately protested, trying to get the key back but he didn't have enough strength. Selena swatted his hand away and started unlocking the chains locking us. I stretched my hands once I was free.

For some reason, I felt bad for Elijah because his so-called friends were just using him because of his position and authority. Only Selena seemed to be loyal to him.

Selena tucked her black hair behind her ear. "There, you're free, please heal him, I can trade his life for mine!"

Still, Caine didn't say anything. He can't be that heartless, can he? I mean, yeah, Elijah locked us up and attacked us, twice, but still.

A little girl went into the room. By what it looks, she's probably about 7 years old. She grumpily hopped onto Selena's side.

"Mom, Gareth stole my doll," she complained.

Selena knelt down so that she was face to face with her daughter. "Heather, you should go back, your dad and I are busy."

Heather pouted, "Hmph! You guys are always busy, I wish I had a mom that spent time with me!" Then, she stomped out of the room. A few moments of silence passed, then a little boy came running over, running around the room while waving a doll above his head. Heather came running just right behind him, trying to reach for her doll.

Selena blocked our view of the kids. "Uhm, please don't mind them, lets go to another room," she offered. She led Caine, Daniel and I to another room, and Elijah stayed in the other room because of being just poisoned, he couldn't walk properly yet. She led us to a room with black walls, it was a small room which seemed to be a place for people to talk in. There were two comfy, small, dark blue chairs with a black pillow neatly placed on it's right side, in the middle of the two chairs was a couch, it was comfy and dark blue, with two pillows on either side of it's ends, just at the side of the armrest.

She sat down on the chair on the right, motioning for us to take a seat. I sat down on the middle couch, and Caine took a seat beside me.

Selena looked at us, then started talking. "Look, the reason why Elijah captured your whole pack was to please his father and also to find a cure to the poison spreading in his body. Yes, vampires, werewolves and witches are the three main supernatural creatures so we are kind of immortal if we don't get killed or something, this poison is made especially for vampires and I researched about it and it's nicknamed 'vampire-killer' because it slowly kills a vampire," she began.

She took a deep breath then continued. "There is no known cure for this poison, it's a poison made especially for vampires, but when witches take this poison, it weakens their magic until they'll eventually have none, only werewolves are immune to this poison, so Elijah's mother think it's made by wolves, also one of the reasons Elijah attacked the wolves, but then again we don't have proof." She finished.

Caine shook his head. "We were the one who made the peace treaty, why would you think we would do that to break it?"

I just stayed silent through their conversation, since I had no part in it.

"Okay, since you aren't the ones who made the poison... We should let you and your pack go, but... I know I'm in no position to ask you this since we were the ones who attacked you for no reason but... Can you try making a cure?"

"I can try, but no promises. Carter is the one good at herbs," Caine replied.

She nodded weakly. "Uhm, I'll ask Elijah to let you pack free since they did nothing wrong, you're free to go now," she said, nodding towards the door. I got up first, very bored of the conversation because I wasn't part of it. I went towards the door but when I opened it, I was tackled to the ground by a vampire.

"Hey!" Selena growled. "You're not allowed to attack anyone without Elijah's or my order or permission!"

But the vampires paid no attention to her, 14 more vampires jumped out of nowhere and attacked us. Caine stepped in front of me and fought off the people who attacked us, I couldn't do much to help, except tell him when someone was attacking from a different direction. I noticed that no matter how intense the fight got, none of them hurt Selena.

Luckily, there were only about 15 members of their coven who were rebelling, and so they were overpowered easily. Other vampires surrounded the vampires who attacked Caine, Selena, and I. Selena looked troubled as she stared at the leader of the rebels. His eyes scanned her body for injuries, when he found none, he exhaled in relief.

"I- I told you to leave me alone," Selena whispered a tiny hint of fear in her voice.

"You chose him instead of me, but we've been together more than you have been with him, I won't give in!"

Chapter 26

"You said you'd respect my decision, whoever I chose," Selena said weakly.

The rebels' leader's eyebrows furrowed. "I only said that because I thought you would choose me, I knew you since we were young, I took care of you when your parents disowned you. Who was with you when your first boyfriend broke up with you? Me! Who was with you when you needed someone to cry on most? Me! I was always there for you. Where was he all those times? Huh?!" His words cut Selena deep, a tear slipped down her eye.

"Look, I'm sorry, it was a really hard decision to make... my mate or my childhood best friend, but you know I can't do that to my mate, I can't live without him!"

"What about me? You can live without me? Have you ever even cared about me?" he whispered the last word out.

This conversation was getting so emotional.

And heartbreaking, my wolf added, pretending to wipe a tear from her eye.

"I did, I- I thought we'd still be friends even though I chose him.." her voice trailed off. "You said-"

"I said all of those because I thought you would choose me instead of him," he growled. "I mean, now he's just a nuisance to you, you're the one taking care of him instead of the other way around. He deserves to be poisoned."

Selena gasped. "L-liam! Were you the one who poisoned him?"

Liam rolled his eyes. "Well? What do you think?"

"Y-you did! It was you!" Selena's shaky voice whispered, she pointed an accusing finger towards his direction.

"You really think I'd take your happiness from you? No, I'm not that cruel."

Selena exhaled in relief, but I still thought it was him who did it. It all adds up. Liam was mad at Selena for choosing Elijah instead of himself, who was with Selena longer than when Elijah was, but they were mates. Liam couldn't bring himself to hurt Selena, so he brought up all his anger mixed with hatred towards Elijah so that if he died, Selena would come crying to him and he would probably take advantage of her vulnerability.

But, of course, being a person who trusts easily, Selena didn't think much about it.

Elijah came limping towards us, but when he saw Liam and Selena in the same room, his fists clenched in a tight ball, trying to contain his anger.

Suddenly, it was like he healed on his own, he rushed towards Selena and started checking and examining her, looking for an injury or bruise. When he found none, he turned around to glare at Liam.

Liam grinned widely. "Oh! It seems like you're already healed. Were you faking it the whole time?"

"I wasn't-"

"Or were you faking it so that Selena would worry about you?"

"I didn't-"

"Enough!" Selena screamed. "If he was faking it, he wouldn't have bothered hiding it from me the first time. And please, please leave me alone Liam."

Liam blinked. He looked hurt. "Well, don't bother asking me for help in the future, if he mistreats you, I will just laugh and blame you for it."

After he said those words, he signaled something I didn't quite understand towards his fellow rebels. They all jumped out of the window. When he was the last one left, he glanced at Selena one last time, then left.

Selena looked at Elijah. "I hope I could get your permission to let the wolves and other vampires free."

He nodded but didn't say anything.

After a few days, we were back at the pack house, with all the other werewolves, they're injuries were treated, and they were well taken care of. Carter was making a cure for Elijah, even though he protested multiple times because of his grudge against vampires.

During these days, Caine and I started growing further apart, I didn't understand why he wanted to stay away from me. Maybe it was because I was a human, and werewolves considered humans as filthy, untouchable beings. Due to having nothing to do, I spent my days reading books about them, I just wanted to fit in.

I was sitting on my bed, reading about how vampires and wolves have been in war for years until they finally made a peace treaty when a knock sounded from my door.

"Come in," I called.

The door opened and Beta Jones went in. He smiled at me warmly before speaking. "We weren't able to do the acceptance ceremony yet, so basically, you and the other humans who turned into werewolves aren't part of the pack yet, we will have the ceremony after two days, I advise you to make some friends before the ceremony so that it will be easier for them to accept you into the pack."

"Oh okay," I said. I would have asked about how it worked but I have already read about this ceremony in a book. He nodded and left.

I sat on my bed, in silence once again, but the silence was short-lived, for, after a few minutes, someone burst into my room, without knocking. A three men went in, followed by two other girls, happily chatting with each other, when they were close enough for me to hear what they were talking about, they stopped talking.

"Uhh, you guys didn't knock," I said, pointing at the now-abandoned door.

"I would, but I was eating Skittles, I might have dropped some," one of the men said as he sucked his chubby finger, which was purplish-red in color, he sucked the flavor out of it and then pointed at the man who opened the door. "Blame him." Then he grabbed another plastic of Skittles and started eating.

When one of the girls tried to grab a Skittle, he swatted her hand away. "Mine."

I stared as they started quarreling, this group sure was a lively one. I watched as they fought over the last plastic of Skittles, how I wish I could be in one of these kinds of groups of friends. But I couldn't fit in nor blend in with the wolves who were born as wolves, isn't that why Caine keeps his distance from me?

If only I could fit in.

Chapter 27

After the group introduced themselves, they excused themselves because they said they had to do something. I didn't get why they even bothered talking to me. I was, after all, a filthy human in a werewolf's eyes. At least I think I was.

The next day was up before I knew it. I tried getting closer to those four amusing friends, turns out, they were the talk of the pack. I found some new things out, like Brody and Ryker being extreme enemies, Brody and his love for Skittles, and other things about Charlotte and Liana.

I went into the dining room lazily, letting the door slam shut softly behind me. I sat beside Brody, he was the easiest to get along with after all. When the pack chef's served the food, Brody immediately leaped on the table and protected the plate of bacons.

"Stop!" He said, pointing his fork at someone who was about to get a piece of bacon. "Mine, mine, mine, mine..."

"You're so annoying," Ryker growled, snatching one of the bacons away from him.

"Ok well, I guess I should leave some space in my tummy for dessert after all," Brody replied, rubbing his stomach.

Maybe not all wolves that were born as wolves were that bad. I guess some could be nice after all. I smiled at Brody, he was the friendliest and the first person who accepted me among the werewolves. I could tell he was favored to be in here, I could tell everyone enjoyed his presence even though some may hide the enjoyment. They enjoyed his childishness and immaturity, only a few people are left with those traits, only some people are left innocent.

Since Brody is eating all the bacons, I decided to just eat pasta. I filled my plate with carbonara and twirled my fork until it was enveloped in pasta. I started eating, wondering if the Alpha's also came to eat in here. Well, no, I was wondering if Caine will eat here. During the past days, I had only eaten in my room, locking myself up, but since I have some friends now, I decided to eat in the dining room, where the pack eats.

I started eating and when I was halfway done, I realized Caine won't be eating here. I had forgotten how I had served him food, personally, and he ate in his room. I wonder who was serving him food right now.

Ezra came running down the stairs, three empty, dirty trays in his hand. "Uhh, is there still food for me to eat?" He glanced on the table, seeing that most of the plates were empty

"Ehm... Brody ate most of everything," Charlotte muttered, pointing at the empty dishes on the table. "But we could ask the pack's chef for the day to get you something to eat?"

Brody gave Ezra a toothy smile. "Sorry dude, I was just too hungry. But I'll spare you some chicken wings for a pack of Skittles?" He offered.

Ezra rolled his eyes. "I don't know where will I even find those stuff, like, do werewolves even eat those?"

"Me, yes. Well, you should have some in your room, it's right in the bin filled with treats. If I knew you hadn't known I would've stolen it." He clamped a hand on his mouth, then spoke again. "I mean it's not considered as stealing, you didn't even know it existed."

"Nah, I'm keeping my Skittles, I'll just ask the pack chef for some food."

"They're shift is done."

Ezra stopped short from his tracks. "What did you just say?"

"Their shift is done," Brody lied again. "So it's either you give me my Skittles or you starve for the night." He faked a serious face.

"Fine. You've got a deal."

This is it. Today is the day I was supposed to be 'accepted' in the pack. Today is the acceptance ceremony. All of the humans were now turned to werewolves, so they didn't have to worry about us running away or disobeying the Alpha's, since if ever we get banned from the pack, we would turn into Rogues.

I have read all about Rogues. They were werewolves who either willingly or forcefully became one, Rogues weren't from any pack, they were lone wolves, and I kind of felt bad for them. They were forced to leave their family when they had to leave their pack, they also had to leave their mates unless they chose to go rogue with him/her. Being a Rogue was deadly, they were a free-for-all kill.

My fingers brushed and pulled the zipper on my back. I was glad I had a long-enough arm to do that. I wore a silver-grey dress, with a pair of matching heels that wasn't too tall as I was not used to wearing heels. I curled and did my hair, I didn't bother putting some make-up on as I never have in my entire life.

Except for when Emma drew lipstick all over my face and made me look like a complete clown.

I sat on the seat, starting at my appearance in the mirror. I looked fine, I guess.

An unfamiliar wolf peeked his head on the door. "The ceremony is starting in 5 minutes, I came to remind you."

I nodded my head in acknowledgment, and he left the room. I grabbed the half-empty bottle of perfume from the table. This had been my childhood favorite, the smell of vanilla and roses. I had put this on almost everyday, which made the scent stick to me even without the perfume, but I sprayed it on anyway.

Wolves I wasn't familiar with led us to double doors, they were made of white wood and was very extravagant. I heard a man say words inside the doors. Then, the doors were opened, and we filled the room one by one, going in by order, by age. The children were up the front, followed by teens and adults. I was the eleventh one in line, and my breath hitched when I saw him.

Caine.

Epilogue

We were seated in the front seats of the large room. I didn't pay attention to what the host was saying. I was focusing on who was going to do the blood pact with us. If it was Caine, it would be terribly awkward as he had been ignoring and staying away from me ever since we came back.

Emma nudged me by the elbow when it was time to line up on the side of the stage. We started going up, one by one, from youngest to oldest. I was now officially nervous. Caine was the one doing the blood pact with the now new pack members since he was the eldest of the three brothers.

I started growing restless as the line started growing shorter, and me being closer to the stage. Ezra was the one before me, and he went up the stage. They just had to repeat the same words all over again. I got more nervous as I walked up the stage. I stood on the opposite side of where Caine was standing, only a tall white circular table in between us. It wasn't like a normal table, it only took up a few inches of space.

We had written out full names just before we had filed into the room, the paper was now on Caine's hands. He hadn't looked up yet, but his eyebrows furrowed when he saw who was next.

Me.

He looked up from the paper.

"Sylvia Harper, do you accept the Cadell brothers as your Alpha?"

Cadell? Sounds weird.

"Yes, I do." Cringe.

"Do you promise to be loyal to this pack, for better or for worse?"

"Yes, I do."

"Let our blood be shared to seal the bond," he picked up a small pocket knife that was on the small white table. It was small but sharp. Very sharp may I add. He slit the knife on his palm, again, then handed it to me.

Stupid werewolf traditions, I don't want to slit my own hand.

But then again, I didn't want to look like a coward. Everyone else would have to do it too anyway. I did it quickly, slitting my own palm and putting it on top of the white table, palm facing Caine's. There was a stone bowl on the table, which had pure water on it. Our blood dripped on it as our palms touched.

It would have hurt, but no, electric tingles shot up my body from where our skin touched. I thought the pain would be there by now, but it felt more pleasurable than pained.

I heard a low growl from Caine's throat. I didn't know what that meant. After our cuts had healed, I went down the stage and sat on my seat. Caine continued to do the same thing to the rest of us.

Brody suddenly popped up to the seat next to me, which is supposedly to be for Emma, who was still on the stage. "Sooo, your Caine's mate, yes?"

Huh?

Yes. My wolf said in my head.

"How did you know?" I asked instead, I was curious on how.

"It was sort of obvious, he was like, growling in pleasure when you two did the blood compact."

I gulped, so that was what it was about. I thought it was because he didn't like making contact with me, since he had been ignoring me after all.

I was bored out of my mind. My wolf kept on bugging me. She was whining on how Caine kept ignoring us, she wanted to be near him, but I knew I couldn't do that.

Charlotte cheerfully went into my room, along with the others. She carefully checked the space between my neck and shoulder but saw no mark on it. "This is weird, mates usually mark their mates as soon as they can, especially Alpha's since they have more urge to do so."

When she saw my face falling, mainly because of my wolf whining, she immediately changed the topic, but I wasn't listening much. I didn't really understand why he was keeping his distance from me, so I decided to ask one of his brothers about this. Onto why he was ignoring me.

I just wanted some sort of clarification, just to shut my wolf up.

So, after leaving and saying goodbye to them, I started making my way up to the 'Alpha's Hall'. Before I could get in, someone stopped me. "No one's allowed to go in without permission."

"Ehm, I just want to speak to-," I began but was interrupted by Caleb's head poking out of the door.

"Let her in."

Thanks for that.

The guard stepped out of my way and allowed me to go in. Caleb relaxed on the creamy couch, resting his head on his hands. "So, what do you want?"

What a nice way to start a conversation.

"Uhm, I'm just curious on why Caine keeps on ignoring me," I said, fiddling with my fingers out of nervousness. I wanted and didn't want to know the answer at the same time. I'm his other half, I deserve to know, right?

What if it was bad, really bad, that I probably would have regretted knowing it?

Caleb saw the mixed emotions on my face and didn't say anything until he saw the pain in my eyes.

"Don't get him wrong, he was ecstatic when he found out he had a mate, I don't know if one of us had mentioned this to you before but we are cursed. We pretty much can't have mates, but even if we did... we'd pretty much go insane once we would mark and complete the mating process with our mates, Caine's the first of us brothers to have a mate so I wouldn't know, but our father had the same condition, so he abused his mate."

I swallowed.

So this was why he kept avoiding me, he didn't want to go insane, didn't want to be crazy, didn't want to hurt me. This curse was the one that was keeping us apart. My wolf wanted to be with him very badly, I had to find a cure before I would go insane because of not being able to be with my mate for too long. Even if it costs my life.

I'll find a cure, but for now, I guess I could live like this for a longer while.